BACK FOR REVENGE

by

Best wishes
Morton Middleditch

Morton Middleditch

Chapter 1

The explosion of thunder overhead brought Bill out of his troubled snooze. He had been dreaming he was dying, which was almost certainly true, but whether he died from the cancer or from a bullet was the part that exercised most of his waking thinking.

The storm had swept in quickly. Before he had dozed of it was a bright windy day, typical of the wide-open Pampas.

Gazing out of the window was one of Bill's greatest pleasures, but then it was a view to behold. Argentina, his home for so long and now the only safe refuge left to him. Elsewhere in the world he was at risk.

January was one of his favourite months. Normally the sun shone brightly in the summer but today the wind had brought the clouds and the rain was now torrential. The rumbles of thunder boomed across the pampas, but the storm was passing as quickly as it had come. He felt tired and he was almost nodding off again when someone entered the room. The clouds were receding. The summer sun was now shining and the air was clear.

"Senor Bill, why you come home?"

"Strange question, as I've been home for three years."

"Don make fun of me, you know what I mean. I your only family now. I first to hold you after you born."

Bill grinned. Angelo Ramirez, 82, not fluent in English but always forthright and stooped after years of hard work but always with a smile. Angelo was his last cherished family, all were dead and some his own doing. His mother had told him Angelo was the first person to cradle Bill in his arms as the doctor passed him over. That was nearly forty years ago. Angelo had been head of the house when family were not around but he had long since passed that job on to his son Emilio. Bill loved him. They were his only remaining family. His English was as faltering now as it was when he had taught Bill to hunt and fish.

"Well Angelo, this is the only home I have left now and so I would, if that is OK with you like to spend all my days here, but only if that is okay with you." The sarcasm was lost on the old man who scuttled off to his favourite place, the kitchen.

Bill wished he could spend the rest of his life in this wonderful place; but that was going to prove most unlikely. Before him was a vast expanse of grassland. To one side of the farm buildings sat the old, somewhat dilapidated family Cessna; an essential tool for getting around in this remote wilderness. In front of him the pampas, his land, spread for fifty miles against the backdrop of the Andes; the magnificence of this part of Patagonia always tugged at his heart when he was away. This had been his great grandfather's home. The old man had settled in Argentina when his whaling ship was wrecked in a terrible storm in 1876. He had decided to stay partly because there was no way to return to England but he had fallen in love and married the daughter of a wealthy Argentinean whose wife was English. They had built up massive estates and the estancia now had twenty rooms and outbuildings to house the hands.

Bill's father had left to go to England after he was born to run other parts of the family's extensive interests but he felt safe here. This had been his other family home where he spent time when business brought him to South America and when he needed to be absent from his other properties in England, Madrid and Lima; homes far away from the modest house in Solihull, the hub where the most lucrative part of the family business had been masterminded. It had made them wealthy but that was all history now. He was a wanted man, his parents and sister dead, the business gone.

Bill Millichip was on the run from police in a number of countries but here in Argentina he still felt safe. Maybe it was the thousands paid to corrupt policemen allowing him to feel so. It could change. Policemen came and went and maybe a new police chief might decide to cash in and turn him over to those who sought him. Everyone could be bought. Who would want him most, Peru, Spain or England?

He put the thought out of his mind. Since the cock up in Peru he had been untroubled at the family Estancia. His life was one of comparative luxury as a farmer with staff, whose loyalty to him had never wavered and he took for granted. Yet something still gnawed at him, unfinished business. He felt alone, denied the companionship of his sister Julia, cut down by a stray bullet from the gun of one of his own men. It had not mattered Julia was not his blood; adopted, he adored her. He felt no remorse in shooting her killer himself, but he also held others responsible.

If only Julia's stupid boyfriend Eddie hadn't stumbled into their camp in Peru looking for her, his problems would not have escalated, but Bill reserved his real hatred for Sam. It gnawed at his senses every waking moment. It was Sam, the policewoman who had befriended Julia to get close to his drug operation; it was she who Bill held to blame and one day she would pay for destroying his family and his business. He rang a bell and within seconds Emilio poked his head round the door.

"Emilio."

"Yes, Bill." Emilio was the only person who could call Bill by his first name. He had earned that right and it suited Bill.

"Find the boys and have them meet me at six o' clock."

"But they are out with the herd. I think they are back tomorrow morning."

"Get one of the hands to bring them in tonight."

Emilio hobbled out of the room to the ranch shed. He had been head gaucho but had been seriously injured in a riding accident and had taken over from Angelo as head of the house. Bill watched him with affection. He had served the family since he was a boy and at sixty performed a valuable service to Bill. He would die here and be buried with other members of the family, his grandfather and his father's two brothers and their wives. Bill hoped he himself would be buried in the plot next to Angelo. The old man had come to him one day and asked for the plot next to a gnarled old yew tree in the corner of the family cemetery. Bill had readily agreed and the look of pleasure on the old man's face was a delight when Bill had told him when his turn came he wished to buried alongside the old man.

Bill sat down in his favourite chair savouring this wonderful view. It was all he had left. The authorities had confiscated the apartments in Peru and Madrid and he had no idea about the house in Solihull. It wasn't he didn't care; there was simply nothing he could do about it. The stress of the last three years had taken its toll and he looked much older than his thirty-nine years. He felt something was wrong. He hadn't seen the family doctor in England for some years and the pains he had been suffering were now getting more intense. The local doctor said it looked like a cancer and the symptoms suggested it might be at an advanced stage. He urged Bill to go to the specialists in the capital for more tests and treatment. So this was the next step and then it would be time to sort out the unfinished business in England. The risks would be great but he felt compelled to take revenge. He closed his eyes and thought about the country he had fled as a fugitive and wondered whether his next decision was really a sensible one to take. He drifted off to sleep.

Emilio tapped his boss on the shoulder and Bill woke with a start. He was always wary, he needed to be; it was part of his life now.

"The men will be back but not before nine, Sir."

Thank you, Emilio. That will be all. Get cook to make some food, they'll all be hungry but we'll look after ourselves this evening."

Emilio left the room. He was anxious. He had been born on the property. His father had been head ranch hand. He had been helping to fetch hot water when Bill was born. Whilst Angelo had taught him to hunt and fish it was Emilio who had taught Bill to ride. His own sons had gone to Buenos Aires preferring to live a different life. They had become part of the political scene and in 1970 became two of the thousands missing as part of the 'Dirty War'. Emilio's wife had died of heartbreak and all that had been left were the Millichips, his other family.

Bill was like a son to him and he owed him total loyalty; he would do anything for him. Emilio had coerced him to go to the doctor on the premise he was ill himself. Bill had taken him to see the doctor unaware there was nothing wrong with Emilio. Bill had laughed at the subterfuge but could not be angry. He knew he should have gone and now he was being sent to see the experts in Buenos Aires. Emilio knew all the family business but his sixth sense detected life, as he had known it for sixty years on this great Estancia might be coming to an end. He had no idea what would then happen to them all.

***

The boys came in prompt at nine. The table had been laid for eight. Bill's gauchos were loyal men. They would die for Bill. They had grown up on the estancia when it was much larger and more profitable than now. Their families had preceded them and they hoped their children would also.

"I've called you back in. I need to talk to you about my plans. Help yourself to drinks and I'll be back in a minute."

He left the room for no other reason than to compose himself and to let the boys relax and settle down. As he walked back in the boys all stood. It was a mark of respect for their boss. It had been accorded to his father and his grandfather and they all knew their lives were dependant on Bill.

"Before we talk let's eat. There are pots of casserole on the heater so help yourselves and the wine is on the dresser." There was a sense of foreboding in the room. This did not happen except at Christmas and where was Emilio?

Pedro, the foreman decided to ask and he spoke in his broken English. "Boss, this is most welcome but also most unusual. Is everything alright?"

Bill replied in fluent Spanish. "We will speak when we have eaten." The meal was a sullen affair with everyone speculating what could be so important they be brought in and provided food in the big house.

At last Bill could bear the silence no longer. "What I have to tell you is that I have to go away for tests. My health is not good. The local doctor says I have cancer and it needs to be treated. He is certain himself but he has no idea how advanced. He says if I don't have treatment then in all probability I will die."

"Boss…"

"Please don't interrupt. This is difficult for me. I am going to Buenos Aires to see a specialist. As you know it is being out here on the pampas that has kept me out of the hands of people who would wish to lock me up. When I came back last time without my parents I told you they were dead. You know I have police protection here but you don't know everything and I'm not about to explain it. Suffice to say without that protection I would have to return to England and I have no idea then what would happen to this family home and to all of you."

Bill looked at the anxious faces around the table. He loved these boys. He had ridden with them as a gaucho and spent some of his happiest days out with them on the pampas and sometimes he felt more Argentinean than British.

"When I go I will put you Pablo in charge of the farm and Emilio in charge of the house. If anything happens to me the property will be held in a legal trust for all of you and your families. A lawyer will come and explain it all to you but you will have rights to live as you do now for as long as you wish. Anyone who leaves the property forgoes his share. Anyone who dies, their share goes not to his wife but to his children."

"Boss…"

"Please Pablo, no questions, not now. The lawyer will explain it but you have a life here as long as you want it. Please continue here, I have to leave tomorrow morning and I have things to attend to."

With that Bill stood and looked at his boys. He left the table wondering if he would ever see them again. After a tearful farewell with Emilio and Angelo, the nearest he had to real family, the next morning he left for Buenos Aires in the old Cessna and was arrested as the plane stopped at a private hanger on the airport. He never found out how they knew he was coming.

Chapter 2

Sam Jacobs turned over as the light shone through the partly open curtain. She lay there warm in the bed, and happy. Happy that life was so good to her. The inner peace she now enjoyed with Eddie and their growing family gave her not only that sense of security she had always craved but also a deep inner satisfaction.

Sam could hear no sounds from the kid's rooms and she always loved Eddie's rhythmic breathing as he lay beside her. She could feel the warmth of his body and it was cosy tucked away from the winter chill outside. She always marvelled that Eddie could sleep most of the night on his back and yet he never snored. His shoulders were outside the covers as he lay on his back. He seemed to have a smile on his face. His eyes were closed and she marvelled at his long eyelashes that most women would die for. They hid his blue eyes that always made her giddy when he looked at her. Even in bed not a hair was out of place; how does he do that she wondered? She could see the pulse beating rhythmically in his neck and felt a deep sense of love for her man. She leaned over and just stared at his handsome face and looked at the scar on his left shoulder. She shuddered at the thought of the bullet smacking into him in the melee that fateful day some five years previously. Fateful, but not in a foreboding way, for it had changed her life forever. The wound had healed but where the bullet entered was part of what he was and a permanent reminder to both of them, which had sealed their life together.

She could not rationalise why she often spent those early moments of the morning remembering the violent manner of their meeting on those mountains in Peru just more than three years previously. She and Detective Inspector Melville had been sent out at the request of the Peruvian police to track a drug trafficking ring run by Bill Millichip. She had befriended a member of the family to get close. She had chosen Julia, Bill's sister who she suspected knew nothing about what was going on and it was the perfect way to get closer to her brother, who the Police believed ran the gang. Little did she know that Eddie would come blundering into the drug traffickers camp searching for Julia and he would be shot and left for dead. She remembered the satisfaction of nursing him back to health and after more trials and tribulations, falling deeply in love with him. On at least two occasions they had nearly been killed. She loved Eddie with an intensity all could see and she was determined to make up for lost time. They conceived the twins before they were married; Rebecca and Holly were now aged three, Mark was now eighteen months and another was well on the way.

To say Sam was happy was an understatement. When she left the Police to start her family she had no idea she would receive the Queen's Commendation for Bravery for her exploits, both in Peru and then back home. Sam's mother had broken down in tears when Sam had told her of the award. Sam knew it would bring back the memories of her father's death. He had been a police officer, shot saving the life of a colleague and had died of his wounds. Sam had been so proud when she and her mother had attended the ceremony where her father had received a posthumous award of the Queens Medal for Gallantry.

There was not a day passed where some part of her meeting with Eddie did not pass through her mind. She was also acutely aware there was still unfinished business. Bill Millichip, who had been responsible for the death of D. I. Melville in Peru and had nearly killed her and Eddie, was still evading capture. She was kept regularly in the picture by former colleagues at New Scotland Yard, but Sam still worried this unfinished business might come and ruin her idyll.

Eddie was awake and he had been looking at Sam. "What are you thinking about? You have that look on your face when something is bugging you."

"Actually, I'm thinking how much I love you and how lucky we are."

"Why the frown then?"

"I can't get Bill Millichip out of my mind. I just know he's out there waiting to spoil my happiness."

"Don't you think he has enough to worry about? He has the Police in South America, Spain and here, all actively searching for him. We get regular reports, so his case hasn't fallen off the radar yet."

"That's the trouble with men."

"What is?"

"Too rational; not switched on to the buggeration factor. If it's out there it can surely bite you when you least expect it."

"Well there's nothing we can do. So why not enjoy what we have."

"Don't think it consumes me all the time. It doesn't."

"Well then."

"Well then what?"

Eddie knew this unfinished business worried Sam but he chose to play it down to show he had every confidence the events in Peru and the immediate aftermath were behind them, although even he had his doubts.

"All I know is that life is almost perfect, darling."

"Almost?"

"Perfect would be a nice cup of tea before I get up to earn us another crust to eat."

Sam poked him in the ribs and then leant over and kissed him on the cheek. She loved the scent of him and wanted to linger but she got out of bed before he could respond. "One cup of tea coming up Sir," and went downstairs pulling on her dressing gown.

Eddie lay there thinking how lucky he was, three children in as many years and one on the way. He loved Sam being pregnant. Her growing lump was the sign reaffirming they were doing what all couples in love do; bring up children with all the pressures and responsibilities that come with it. He didn't believe he could feel so happy.

He had long got over Julia, the cause of Eddie and Sam meeting in the first place. Julia was Bill Millichip's adopted sister although he didn't know it at the time and Eddie's girlfriend although he certainly had no idea the family was in the drugs business. Neither had Julia, or so he'd been led to believe. Julia was now dead, killed by members of Bill's own gang when she had tried to stop Eddie being murdered. He found he hadn't grieved as he might have expected. Perhaps being shot in Peru by Julia and being left for dead had something to do with it. Eddie had chosen to put her right out of his mind.

Life had been good for Eddie since that episode in Peru. Despite long periods away from his work, Vince, the owner of the consultancy business, had appointed Eddie as chief executive and given him some shares. So he was now a wealthy man but he willingly felt indebted to Vince for his patience, understanding and support. Vince was like a father to him. Vince's business was Eddie's only job since leaving University and the two had become great personal friends. The foundation of this friendship had been laid when Vince's wife had died of cancer some years previously and Eddie helped him run both his family and the business whilst Vince was consumed by grief.

Despite the difficulties Eddie's long absence from work had caused Vince, it had never put a permanent strain on their relationship. Quite the reverse, Vince became convinced Eddie was the man to take over the reins when he wanted to step back. Eddie felt indebted and apart from two occasions when he thought he might have to resign in order to have time to search for Julia, he had become convinced his 'home' was with Vince. Eddie was loyal and there was a debt to be repaid although Vince never made it seem that way.

The tea arrived at the same time as the twin's. Rebecca and Holly came noisily to disturb Eddie's thoughts of the past. Sam lifted them onto the bed for their morning cuddle. Eddie made it a rule every business day he would always see the children in the morning before going to the office and in the evening before they went to bed. Sam looked on with great satisfaction at the scene but was jolted sharply by baby Mark who had started crying. Although he was only eighteen months old, he knew what was happening and hated being left out of family cuddles. Sam scooped him out of his cot and brought him in and gave him to Eddie.

She always felt emotional at times like this. It was emotion brought about by her state of happiness and the bulge; somehow she felt guilty she could feel this happy. She went downstairs to prepare the breakfast. It was only then she realised it was Saturday. Saturday was Eddie's turn to get an early cup of tea. She had fallen for it again; she didn't mind and busied herself.

The post arrived and there was an envelope with bold red printing 'Do not bend'. She opened the envelope there were a number of photos in mounts. The return address on the envelope showed they had been sent by Detective Inspector George Strachan at New Scotland Yard. The note said simply 'Sorry it has taken so long to get these to you. Okay for lunch next Wednesday? Ring.'

These were the photos of Sam receiving the Queen's Commendation for Bravery, nearly two years previously. The picture she most liked was that taken with her mother with Eddie and George. She was fond of George. He had never been her direct boss but had always looked out for Sam. It was George Strachan whose life had been saved by Sam's father. It was for this act of heroism Sam's father had received his Medal. An armed gang had shot George in the leg as they attempted to shoot their way out of a Post Office. George had lain injured in the direct line of fire, unable to move. It had been a vicious shoot out which had seen saw all four gunmen eventually killed by police marksmen. Whilst under constant fire Sam's father had tried to drag George out of the line of fire; as he did so he was shot in the back and died but not before he had dragged George to safety.

Sam had decided to leave the force when she met Eddie and had not regretted it at all. Sam's mum was pleased she had chosen marriage as the alternative to police work. She had lost the only man in her life and she did not want to lose her only daughter. She had never put Sam under pressure even when she had given up her original nursing career to join the Police; she deliberately never ventured her opinion on the subject. She was not that sort of mother; anyway she had always found her suggestions to Sam usually brought the opposite response; that was the way Sam had been all through her adolescent life; headstrong.

Eddie came downstairs with Mark in his arms and Rebecca and Holly making their way behind him, sliding from step to step. Eddie was wearing his tracksuit bottoms and the faded tee shirt on which were the words 'I survived the Inca Trail' was stretched across his chest. Countless washings had made it fade and he must have put on weight, it seemed much tighter. It was the tee shirt Sam had bought him in Peru after they had struggled down from Machhu Picchu. Eddie had worn it deliberately to remind Sam he would never forget but for her he'd be dead.

"Look Eddie, here are the photos of the award ceremony. I thought we'd never see them."

They looked at them together. Eddie felt enormous pride seeing his wife receiving such a prestigious honour. "I tell you what. We must have a lunch party and get your mum, Vince and George down to celebrate."

"That's a great idea, I'll get on it."

Eddie watched the girls tuck into breakfast; and Sam feeding Mark between his loud giggles.

"I'm going to see George for lunch at New Scotland Yard in a couple of weeks. I'll set it up then. I'll get some dates from your secretary. I'll take the kids to mum's and I'll talk to her and George about the date then. You won't mind if we include Juan Ramos will you?"

"No, of course not." Eddie was only too aware that he owed Juan a great deal. It was Juan who had saved Sam's life when she had gone back to investigate the death of Melville. Juan Ramos was now seconded from the Peruvian Government to liaise with the Police in London on drugs being brought in from Peru. Eddie had met him frequently and liked him.

"I'm just going out for a run. Look at this tee shirt – I must be putting on weight. I'll only be half an hour. It looks too bleak to be out longer." Eddie hated jogging but felt he needed the exercise. In fact he'd remained exactly 12 stone, the same he was when he met Sam.

"You haven't had your breakfast. Don't go out without putting on another layer," but Sam was already talking to a closed door; he was off.

The phone startled her.

"Hi Sam. This is George."

"What's up? We're seeing each other soon aren't we? I've just seen the photos. I'd forgotten all about them."

"Sam, I thought you might want to hear this. Bill Millichip had not left Argentina. He was arrested in Buenos Aires."

"That's weird. Eddie and I were just talking about Bill. Does that mean we can extradite him?"

"We have to fight the Peruvians for that right but the Embassies have talked and they probably won't object."

"When will he be brought back?"

"Not sure at the moment."

"You will tell me as soon as you know."

"Of course. One thing I can tell you. PR department have said already they want to do a piece on you and your Gallantry award and this is the hook. The capture of Millichip should bring the whole sorry story to an end. They've asked me to set it up. Our boys should go out to Buenos Aires all being well within a couple of weeks and bring him back."

"George, I'm not too keen to go back over this. There are things I don't want to say; things even Eddie doesn't know."

"I can't force you but I think you should. If it helps I'll say you'll only do it if I sit in, I'll ensure you don't get pushed too far."

"OK but I'm not happy."

"Look, see it from our point of view. This is a case being wrapped up after four years and it's a great story. Police morale will be boosted and our image definitely could do with a polish. Trust me, it'll be fine."

"For you, I'll do it. Let me know when. I'll need to jot down what happened and when."

"OK Sam, I'll be in touch. Bye for now and don't worry."

Chapter 3

Sam went to Scotland Yard strangely excited at the prospect despite her earlier fears. It was a good story and out of it had come life with the man she adored and a family. Life couldn't be better and yet as far as she knew until George's call, Bill Millichip had still been on the run and could have been here in England. So now the end might be in sight. He was under arrest but still fighting extradition. She would not rest until he was in prison. She met George at the reception and he took her along to an office where the police journalist and a photographer were setting up.

"This is Sam Jacobs. Sam let me introduce you to Veronica Pellew and John. John would like a few pictures and then will go and we have as much time as you need."

"Hi. I wasn't sure I wanted to do this but George is so persuasive. So let's get on with it."

The photographer busied himself taking formal and casual shots of Sam on her own and with George and then left. They settled in the armchairs provided in the Press area and Veronica set out the process. "I want to chat informally and let you tell the story. I'll prompt from what I know from the files but it is your story. The readers of the magazine are all in the force so they're not bothered with police procedure, so let it be nice and light."

"It's not a particularly light story."

"OK Sam, it's yours to tell."

The phone on the desk rang. Strachan picked it up. "Yes Gemma, can it wait?" He listened for a moment and said, "I'll be out straight away."

"Sorry ladies but I'll be a few minutes. Carry on without me if you want to." He rushed out of the room and Sam wondered what had been so important.

"I'm happy to start." She settled into the chair as the door closed behind Strachan. She had already decided there were a number of areas she wouldn't cover. She hadn't told Eddie so she wasn't about to tell the world. Killing someone, even if they were about to kill you, wasn't something to brag about. George had agreed it was best left untold, although Veronica had access to the files so she might ask. George had pre-warned her some subjects were off limits but no doubt her journalist instincts would prove too strong on such a tasty morsel.

"Tell me in your own words how you came to be involved in the Peru project?"

"I had been moved into the Drugs Squad a few months earlier and I was chosen in order to try to get close to Bill Millichip who was known to be involved in a drugs ring based on his parents' home in Solihull."

"What do you mean get close to?"

Sam was wary of the question. She had no intention of saying how she had befriended him and the menace she detected in Bill's manner. Nothing was going to be told she would have trouble talking to Eddie about. She ignored the question and continued.

"Befriend him or as it turned out his sister Julia so we could know more about his movements, particularly as we suspected he would be going back to Peru. He'd made a number of regular visits and we knew the family had connections in Spain and Argentina as well as Peru. It was a secret assignment and I understand it had Foreign and Home Office approval. I certainly got the impression it went up to the top for authority. I met Bill Millichip but actually became friendly Julia who asked me to accompany her to Peru on holiday after her break-up from her boyfriend."

"That's Eddie, your husband."

"Yes."

"Sorry, I didn't mean to break your train of thought."

George came back. He looked flushed. Sam wondered whether she should ask him what had happened but she knew he wouldn't say in front of Veronica.

"Julia and I went to Peru and were looked after by what I now know were definitely members of the drugs ring. We went up to near Machu Picchu by a back route to keep out of the way of the authorities. We believed this was the start point of a drugs route for cocaine into England."

"Was it?"

"Not in any big way but it was certainly part of their drugs empire."

"What happened next?"

"I think Bill was on to me and one day we were up in the mountains in camp deep in jungle. We had heard some gunshots earlier and everyone was edgy. All of a sudden Eddie blundered into the camp. After a great deal of shouting, Julia panicked and for some reason picked up a gun on the table, Eddie was shot in the shoulder."

"Why did she do that? It's a bit odd to shoot your boyfriend."

"Ex-boyfriend. Anyway it was Bill who was shouting for her to shoot. Julia was wrecked after the break-up, highly stressed and emotional, crying at the slightest thing. Everyone was jumpy and Bill thought the police might be coming. Julia suddenly picked up the gun from a table. She had the gun in her hand. It was waving about all over the place. She couldn't have shot him if she'd tried but Bill lunged to grab it and it went off. As Eddie fell to the ground I ran out of the camp. I was certain Bill would turn on me. I was right. He sent someone after me. I had feared this and worked out a number of hiding places."

"Did they find you?"

Sam thought about the lie she wanted to conceal. It was on the police record but she hadn't even told Eddie. When the thug had found her he had tried to rape and kill her but she had managed to shoot him with his own gun in the struggle. It had gone off as he pinned her down. "No, I was too well-hidden. Nobody else came so I assumed they thought I had been killed."

Sam could see Veronica was less than convinced but was pleased when she decided not to push the point.

"They all cleared out of the camp and when I returned I found Eddie bleeding badly. They'd left him for dead. Probably Julia had pleaded with Bill not to kill him. He was bleeding so he would have died eventually. I had been a nurse so I patched him up and eventually got him down the mountain. It took more than a week. We were treated like royalty and repatriated to England."

"What do you mean 'like royalty'?

"Nobody asked what I was doing on the mountain although I expect the Embassy had been told and Eddie had left the group he had gone up the mountain with using a false permit so he thought he'd be in trouble. We were put up in a swish hotel and sent back Club Class to England."

"What happened back in England?"

"I said goodbye to Eddie, debriefed my boss."

"That was Detective Chief Superintendent Callaghan."

"That's right." Sam wondered how she would tackle his part in this story. If asked she would tell but maybe the authorities did not want to rake over the mess of police corruption. "I was told the other officer D.I. Mellville from West Midlands Force who had gone separately under cover to Peru had been murdered, almost certainly by Bill Millichip so I asked to go out to investigate and bring his body home. He was a fine officer and although I only met him once I liked him."

"What happened when you went back?"

"Police corruption was rife in Peru but there was one officer I grew to trust. His name is Juan Ramos and he saved my life when I was abducted and about to be murdered by Bill Millichip's people on the police payroll."

"Juan is over here seconded to our force. Did you have any part to play in this?"

"I'd like to think I was the catalyst. Juan's father was a policeman. He fought corruption and was killed and almost certainly the same would have happened to Juan. When you're close to death and someone intervenes and nearly loses his life in doing so, a bond forms between you. My father was a policeman who died in service saving someone who is now my closest friend."

"George Strachan."

"Yes." Sam glanced at George and was sure his lip was quivering. She looked away.

"Let's get back to Peru. How were you abducted?"

"I was resting on my bed in my hotel and I heard a knock and a voice said 'room service'. I was half asleep and was about to shout out when I felt a hand over my mouth and then I remember nothing till I woke up in a barn."

"So what happened then?"

"A policeman I had seen before was standing over me with a gun and a figure who I couldn't make out was standing off to the side. They were discussing in Spanish who was going to kill me. Just as he was about to shoot, a shot was fired. The man standing over me had been shot by someone else who I couldn't see. That was Juan Ramos who had trailed the men. So he saved my life but he was then shot himself. Juan had already radioed in for the cavalry to come and as they arrived the other man ran off. Juan said that man was his boss."

"My God. I had no idea when I was briefed that so much had happened."

"There's more. Once back in England I debriefed Callaghan, my boss, and had a few days off. I had been thinking about Eddie and wanted to find out how he was."

"Had you fallen for him by this time?"

"Oh yes. I'd fallen for him nursing him after the shooting. I knew then that would be it."

"What do you mean?"

"That we'd become an item. It was just a matter of when. I didn't know the details but after we got back he was arrested when he went to Julia's parents to tell them about Julia. Julia's parents were missing and they were later found murdered. The police suspected Eddie was involved having followed Julia to Peru but Eddie had no idea a drugs ring was based on that house and the family were all involved."

"Including Julia?"

"I don't think so. Certainly not before she went to Peru. But there can be no doubt afterwards she must have known and when it turned out that she had been adopted by the Millichips and her real father was my boss Callaghan, it's difficult to work out whether she knew or not. She's dead so we'll never know."

"Tell me about her death?"

"Firstly let me say I liked Julia. I personally think she was not involved but just caught up in the family's mess. They, and by that I mean Bill Millichip with Callaghan's connivance, abducted me and took me to a farm in Surrey. There they planned to kill me. They forced Julia to ring Eddie to come and she knew he would. When he got there he knew he'd been suckered and Bill tried to kill us both but in a shootout, Julia was shot and killed by one of his own men. Bill went wild. He totally lost it and set fire to the barn with Eddie and me and Julia's body inside. Eddie got us out, including Julia at great risk to himself and he suffered burns. We were taken to different hospitals. Me to London and Eddie to Guildford for treatment of his burns, but he was only in a couple of days. I was suffering from trauma but wanted to go home. Unfortunately another bent copper had me abducted on the orders of Callaghan and I was taken to a house in Cricklewood. Eddie came to visit me at the hospital immediately after the abduction and instigated a search. He mistrusted the police so he got in touch with his mate's girlfriend, Lizzie. She was a resourceful and well-connected lawyer, the goddaughter of a Deputy Chief Constable. She hired a lovely private eye who tracked me down and rescued me. This was all down to Eddie's persistence. Callaghan fled as the net closed in."

"What then?"

"Well, as you know, Callaghan is dead; committed suicide before he could be captured."

"Yes, I knew but I suspect that won't feature in the story."

"That's it really. Eddie and I set up home immediately and I fell pregnant, and that was three, no more than three years ago. But for the Queen's medal it would all be history, filed away forever as I would have preferred."

"Anything you want to add?"

"No, I don't think so, thanks. When will it appear?"

"Within the month. I've got loads more from the files but the conditions are that George and his boss have to approve it before publication so I'm not about to step out of line."

George smiled like a father watching over his daughter. "I'll make sure it's okay Sam. It won't embarrass you or Eddie."

"There was one thing. Eddie was badly dealt with by the police when he was arrested and…"

"Sorry Sam but we're not going there. Off limits." George looked at her sternly. Sam knew there was no use arguing.

Sam and George said goodbye and left the room together whilst Veronica packed up her tape machine. They sat in George's office.

"How do you think it went?"

"From your point of view fine. I think Veronica will try to add in some bits we shall want to exclude. We won't want to go over police corruption in our force so we'll have to do some editing."

"George, can I see it before it goes out?"

"Why?"

"There are things I've not told Eddie. He has no idea I shot that man who tried to rape me. Also I've never been too keen to talk about how I came to know Julia or how I used her to get closer to Bill."

"I'll let you see it but you can't change anything. What you will have to do is to decide how much you need to come clean about."

"Fair enough. I'll be off now. Got an anti-natal check later this afternoon."

"Do you know what it is?"

"It? I don't but it's another boy. Trust me. Mother's instinct."

"Got a name?"

"Yes, John George Edward after the most important men in my life."

"Could have called him 'Juan'."

"Nah. Not a good idea. He'll know and if he doesn't work it out I'll tell him."

"Well I'm chuffed to bits. Thanks Sam."

"Don't know what I'll do if it's a girl. Have to be Georgie." She was about to leave and remembered the phone call George had taken. "What was the phone call? Seemed urgent."

"It was. I'm afraid there may be issues over Millichip's extradition. Appears he has cancer and their Courts may not be so keen to offload him in that state. So we have to wait and see what happens. Our boys are on the way there. They'll report back."

"I'd prefer him to die locked up for the killings than die of cancer. Still being off the streets is what we must hope for."

"We've stood down your protection unit. So that's good news for you. You're free to go about safely."

"I suppose. Okay Bye for now, speak soon. Any news you'll let us know? Promise."

"Promise."

Chapter 4

Jamie peeked out of the window of his flat into the dark, cold night. Tooting wasn't a bad place but bad things happened to him there. He suspected something might happen that night; more often than not it did, some niggle or other. He never seemed able to venture beyond the confines of his safe haven; his little second floor flat, without something or somebody dumping on him. It never ceased to amaze him how trouble found him. His trip was essential; could not be delayed. His fridge was empty. The local Convenience store beckoned for milk, bread and eggs, at the very minimum.

He had spent much of his life suffering at the hands of bullies and low life thugs. In the last year particularly he'd come to accept it as the norm, so he now ventured out with increasing rarity. He blamed the whole world, with one exception, his mother. He had adored her. He never knew his father. His father had left as soon as she had become pregnant. It didn't bother his mother and when he was old enough to understand she used to hug Jamie, "We are better off without him," she always said if he raised the subject, "we're happy and we get by, don't we?"

He was always happy to agree. It wasn't he was fooling himself just to please her. He had no feelings at all for his father; he didn't even know his name. He had never seen him; he had never contributed to his life in any way whatsoever. Jamie was the only one in his class at school who did not have two parents. It seemed to him most had parents who were separated and he could see the unhappiness of those kids and somehow he felt better off, not being torn between two warring adults. His mother was always there for him.

It had been tough enough not to have a Father. Jamie had been conscious enough he was not the prettiest child. He had large ears and endured endless Dr Spock taunts; followed by 'beam me up Scotty' as he walked by. To cap it all he had crooked teeth. There seemed a dearth of National Health dentists and no money for private treatment to correct the problem. It had upset his mother.

His nicknames were numerous; but it was his small size right through his school days that was the worst burden. He never made that growing spurt as he went through puberty and he had been picked on. The easiest route for Jamie had been as a loner and concentrate on his studies; but that only led to him becoming the class nerd. Jamie felt life was so unfair, as he was to find out with monotonous regularity through his later years.

Jamie only found out what his Mother did for work as she neared death from cancer. He had been just sixteen when she had come to his bedroom as he was doing his homework in his final year at school. She had opened his door and they sat together on his bed. To Jamie, his mother was an angel. He idolised her so it was the cruellest of shocks to hear she had cancer and it was terminal. She laid the facts out so plainly.

"Jamie, you know I've not been feeling too good for some time."

"Yes Mum, what did the doctor say?"

"Well, I had some tests and they say I have cancer of the liver."

"Can it be treated? They have wonderful treatments now," he said trying to put a brave face on it. His intuition was at play; he knew there was worse to come.

"I'm afraid not darling. This is very advanced and they say treatment is unlikely to be successful."

"But…"

"Listen carefully. I know it's unfair but I really can't go through the pain of treatment if at the end I'm likely to go anyway. It may sound selfish but if my time's up I would rather not prolong the agony. I think it is best for you as well."

"You can't mean that. It's not best for me. I want you to live forever and what if they're wrong and you could be cured." Jamie had grown angry and he didn't want to be. That was it. He was going to lose the one thing he loved. He had only been sixteen, it wasn't fair. Nothing had prepared him for this shock. For him, home was the only place he felt safe.

"Darling, I…"

"How long have you got mum?" Jamie was trying to be brave but was in turmoil inside.

"Only months." She had tried to say it as gently as she could but there was nothing she could do to ease his anguish.

He had sat there in stunned silence for a moment, but he wanted to be strong for her. He was searching for something comforting to say but his mind was in a fog. He was speechless. They sat together holding hands in the sanctuary of his bedroom. Until that moment it had been the place he could hide from the world; hide from all the unhappy things that happened to him. Now she had violated this one area where he was safe. He felt anger welling up inside him. He knew it was not her fault; but to have told him in his bedroom had been an intrusion; she could have told him in the lounge. Later he wondered why at this time he asked his next question.

"Mum, where did the money come from for us to live here?"

She smiled at him as she squeezed his hand. She was not embarrassed.

"I had started to earn money for the two of us by working in a strip club. I had no money from your father and I would not have taken it if he had offered. Stripping did not meet the bills and so I had become a call girl. Do you know what that is?"

"Not exactly, isn't it a kind of prostitution?"

She smiled at how grown up he appeared to be. She was not going to dress it up for him She told him the truth without innuendo, no room for misunderstanding, almost brutal in her frankness.

"Sort of, but I never worked on the streets; I could not have coped with that," she had told him looking straight in to his eyes, "it was better; no, classier and it paid well." His Mother elaborated a little, sparing him the unnecessary details, only wanting to reassure him of her deep love for him.

Jamie had not asked any more questions. He couldn't speak. She had left him in his room to allow him time to formulate anything he might want to ask. Jamie had cried the moment she had walked out, grieving for a mother to be lost and worse, to be lost in a very short space of time. He could not bring himself to reproach her for doing what she did to keep them together and for loving him as she did. He loved her more than ever and she was going to be stolen from him.

The next few days had passed in a blur and for the next few months they spent all the time they could with each other. The end had come more quickly than she had expected. The disease was rampant and she was in increasing pain, but refused to go to hospital. Their family doctor, a kindly old man, who must have been near retirement, did all he possibly could to relieve the pain. It was clear from the Doctor's manner the end for her would be much quicker than she'd been led to believe. In the weeks leading up to her death she told Jamie she had saved quite a sum of money, which would more than see him through till he finished his education.

"I want you to go to University after you finish school. I have saved quite a large amount, but I want you to go and live my sister until you go to University."

Jamie had spurned the offer to go and live with his aunt. He didn't care much for her and he reassured his mother he was going to carry on alone. He asked only sufficient questions to enable him to plan for his future; but the priority was nursing her in her final months.

***

How much water had passed under the bridge since then? He was now thirty-five years old. Little wonder he failed all his exams; what did he care, it was nothing compared to losing the only thing in his life that mattered. He became streetwise and was financially secure for a young man. He decided never to put roots down. Not for him settling down in one place and buying a property. He lived in rented flats but he made them a comfortable and safe haven from the bad things happening around him.

Jamie's real problem was his attitude and his background. He was only five foot three inches tall; the loss of his mother and early life at school had left him with an outsize chip on his shoulder. For many years he had wondered how people dealt with bullying. He had gone onto chat lines and it seemed to him the commonest answer was to confront bullies. That was okay unless you really were on your own; without back up or support it seemed to him a lost cause. He was a real loner; somehow he now preferred it that way.

Thinking of that torrid time he had forgotten he needed to go shopping. February was as usual a harsh month; the winter had been long and drawn out. Darkness at five o' clock was very depressing and the promise of spring so far away. The wind, a permanent feature of the last few weeks, was howling round the corner of the street as he walked to the Convenience store. He only shopped at this one store. It had everything he needed, even if it did cost a little more. He could be in and out within five minutes if he picked the right time. Everything else came from purchases on the web, so he had no need to go out into hostile environments; those, which were unknown to him and worse, those that were.

Jamie turned the corner and right in his path a gang of three in hoodies were bending over something on the pavement. It looked like a rag doll the way it was being kicked around. They were beating up a young lad, kicking and punching him; he lay on the ground unable to stop the torture. Jamie felt for him but his instinct was to pass by. He had no desire to stop or attract their attention. But something stopped him in his tracks. The young lad was looking directly at him through eyes half closed from the beating. Their eyes met; the look on the young boy's face was pleading for help, but no cry for help could pass his bruised lips.

Jamie did something quite alien to his nature.

"Leave him alone," he shouted with as much conviction as he could find. He waited for a reaction and got it. The kicking and punching stopped.

"What did you say, squat face?" The one in the centre who had been inflicting most of the punishment stood back and fixed his stare on Jamie. He noticed the boy on the floor get up and hobble away.

Now Jamie, the centre of attention, the target. He turned to run but was totally unprepared for the punch that felled him to the pavement. He had been hit by a fourth thug who had been keeping a watch in case the police had come along. Jamie was winded and fighting for air. His mind could not focus on what had happened; as he lay there gasping for air he heard a voice urging more violence. He could see all the gang had now gathered round him.

"Kick him." The voice sounded primeval.

"Let him see what's coming first." The mist cleared and Jamie could only see three youths but there may have been more. There was at least one more as he was kicked in the kidneys from behind. He yelled with pain. The pain was intense. It was quite unlike pain he had experienced in beatings before. He stayed down but that did not stop the onslaught. Kicks were aimed only at his body. It was as though they were intent on causing no damage that could be seen by anyone who found him. He was kicked repeatedly around the lower back.

Then, as suddenly, brutally as it had started, it stopped. He heard the sound of them running away. He had no idea why, he didn't care. He was just relieved; he hurt all over his body but his face was not touched. He became aware a car had stopped at the curb and heard a voice.

"You all right mate? They've gone. Do you need help?"

These were the kindest words anyone had spoken to him for years; he looked around and the lad he had gone to help was nowhere to be seen. 'So much for trying to help', Jamie thought. He looked at the driver; he had not bothered to get out of the car.

"Yeah, can you drop me at the Police Station?"

There was a pause. "Sorry mate, I'm going the other way." The man wound up the window and drove off. That was it. It wasn't convenient so he just left Jamie lying on the pavement.

"So much for the kind thought." Jamie said out loud; but there was nobody to hear. Just the disappearing red tail lights of the car and lights of the Convenience store fifty yards away, flickering through the branches of a tree in the cold night air.

Jamie got to his feet. It hurt; it hurt like no other pain he had ever suffered. At these times of stress he often thought of his mother and he thought to himself his pain was nothing to the pain she had endured as the cancer ate away at her. He hobbled back to his flat. He was almost glad there was nobody else around to witness his predicament.

He reached his flat and lay on the sofa catching his breath. He was finding it hard to breathe since he had climbed the stairs. He stripped off his jacket and shirt. The angry red wheals on his back were painful now but what they would be like in the morning he didn't dare contemplate. He knew he needed to be checked out. He rang for a mini cab from the unit next to the Convenience store.

"Hello, can you collect me from flat 3, second floor of Howard House please. I need to go to the A&E Hospital."

"Five minutes, okay? Ahmed is just on his way back in. He's the nearest."

"Okay, thanks. I'll be in the lobby on the ground floor."

"Right."

Ahmed was there in two minutes. He was a cheery guy. Full of chat, which was not what Jamie needed. "To A&E mate, is that right?

"Yeah."

"What do you want to go there for?" Ahmed enquired cheerily.

"Just visiting a friend." He was not in the mood to explain his beating.

He was at the A&E entrance within 10 minutes. He paid Ahmed and walked in to find the waiting area was full. It was Friday evening, the busiest night of the week. He went up to reception.

"Can I help you?"

"I need to see a doctor. I've been beaten up and kicked in the back."

The receptionist hardly looked up and started writing notes on a form.

"Name?"

"Jamie Smith."

"Address?"

Jamie started to give his address but wanted to know how long he might have to wait.

"Friday is as you can see a very busy time. Once I've completed this form then you can sit somewhere and you'll be called."

"But how long might that take."

"Between two and four hours. There are people with serious injuries in here so you won't be a priority."

'How did she know?' thought Jamie. He looked around and there were people with head wounds. Friday night fights in the pub. He decided he wasn't going to get any priority and on the spur of the moment walked out into the cold night air.

Ahmed was still outside hoping for a fare so he got back in the Cab.

"Quick visit," he quipped. "Where next, back home?"

"No. The police station, please."

This caught Ahmed by surprise. He must have wondered why, but decided to say nothing and drove to the nearest police station. Jamie got out of the cab. The pain was now getting worse.

"You alright mate? You look a bit rough."

"Sorry, long story. How much?"

He paid and rounded the fare up to a fiver.

"Cheers mate."

Jamie gathered himself to explain the night's events. He walked in to find yet another queue.

Jamie looked at the queue. 'This is a conspiracy,' he thought. Nobody looked at him as he joined the end behind a girl with a torn skirt; there must have been twenty people jostling for attention around the desk where a policeman was laboriously taking details with a pencil. Everybody in the queue was concentrating on getting to the front, all thinking his or her problem more important than anyone else's. There were angry exchanges as one elderly man shoved his way to the front. Jamie thought this was hopeless; he made his decision to leave. It wasn't he couldn't be bothered. If he did stay at least the Police would have to record the incident. He could give no description of the thugs so it was unlikely they would take direct action. He felt in some way he owed the young lad a report but then again he had skipped off once the attention had turned from himself to Jamie.

It was something else that made him walk away into the cold night air. In an instant he had seen the futility of complaining. Had he done so and the thugs had by some miracle been caught it might make life impossible living where he was. The one good thing about his loner existence was he liked where he lived. It was no seedy bed-sit one might expect one of life's failures to live in. His apartment was just how he wanted it. His landlord never ventured near him and Jamie gave no cause for complaint about his tenancy. It was modern and sparsely furnished. He had electronic gadgetry for drawing the blinds, a security camera, a large Plasma TV, his music and computer. It was his bolthole from a world against him.

If he antagonised the low life that had beaten him up, he might be forced to move and that he could not entertain as an outcome of the night's terror. No, something else had made him walk out of the police station. He decided as a result of his wasted visits that evening he would start to take control of his own life. He had never got much from relying on others; this would be the time, he would deal with this himself. He would exact revenge in some way. He had no plan; it was more an instinct that made Jamie decide to take action himself.

Chapter 5

The two detectives touched down in Buenos Aires after the gruelling flight from Heathrow. It had landed for an hour at Sao Paulo but travelling economy they had been cramped and uncomfortable. They expected an upgrade on the way back with their prisoner, Millichip; a nasty thug by all accounts, but first they had all the legal paperwork to deal with.

The taxi drove into the city down wide streets but the place looked down beat. There were no grand buildings to speak of and they drew up outside the Intercontinental Hotel.

Andy said to his boss, "The flight might have been crap but at least we've got nice digs."

Detective Sergeant Billy Day reflected on a number of similar extradition assignments. They were all the same. Going was awful but coming back was usually much better. "Andy, when you've done this a few times it's just another day in the office. It's just a different office."

They had little luggage and were quickly checked into adjoining rooms overlooking the city with no particular landmark to speak of. The concierge had taken them personally to their rooms. George reflected that usually this was the responsibility of the porters; then again when the Chief of Police personally rang and made the booking it rather suggested it might pay to be extra attentive.

Despite Billy's comments D C Andy Pride was nevertheless overawed by the fact he had been chosen for this assignment and although they only expected to be away for a few days he was determined to make the most of it. He took a beer from the fridge and took a long swig. It tasted good after all the coffee on the flight. James had told him not to drink too much on the flight. He hadn't wanted his partner pissed if they had any business to transact on arrival.

A message light was illuminated on his phone and Billy dialled the message service. A voice in broken English said they would be collected in the morning at 09.00 hours and taken to Police Headquarters. The contact name was 'Ramirez'.

He knocked on the adjoining door and suggested they went to stretch their legs, get an early meal and turn in by early to be ready for the big day. If things ran true to form they would not see Millichip immediately. The paperwork would be submitted for scrutiny and the necessary authority for extradition would be issued. It turned out recently there had been big changes in the Police force in Argentina and Millichip could no longer rely on their cooperation. It seems they were happy to have him off their patch.

Promptly at nine the next morning, the phone rang and their driver was waiting downstairs. The drive to headquarters did not take long despite the heavy traffic; something to do with the blaring police siren.

They were ushered into a dingy office, stale with cigar smoke and greeted by an Englishman from the Embassy who was present to help translate and serve the papers. Billy was pleasantly surprised at this unexpected cooperation, which he neither expected nor had experienced before. There was little for him and Andy to do. The Embassy man, whose name he hadn't caught, but didn't want admit so, was super-efficient and handed over the documents and spoke in fluent Spanish. The whole thing took less than five minutes.

"That's it. The extradition hearing is agreed within the week. Flights will be confirmed by the Embassy with BA. I'm told you had open returns but as you are on 'diplomatic business' we will handle your flights."

"That's fine with us. The sooner we are back the better. The proceedings against Millichip are long overdue."

"One thing you may not know is that Mr Millichip is not a well man. We think he has been diagnosed with cancer which is at quite an advanced stage."

"How long is he expected to live?"

"No idea. He was coming to town to see specialists."

"If he dies quickly it will upset a lot of people who want Millichip to pay for the killing of D I Melville in Peru."

"That's not my problem. I'll do anything you need of me to ensure he leaves Argentina in accordance with the warrant."

"Understood and thanks. When can we see him?"

"He has to be signed off by a Judge in Court; purely a formality. They've had him for a few days. There's been a delay in getting a Judge. Only the most senior judges can deal with this. I guess his lawyers pulled strings to delay whilst they fight the extradition. You are not allowed to interrogate him here in the cells below until the extradition is agreed. I will accompany the police to Court but I suggest you are not present. Judges can get touchy about extradition here and I don't want him taking offence to either of you." The Embassy official sensed a reaction was coming from the detectives, "Just being cautious, that's all. You will be told when to report back here. I suggest you do some sightseeing. Buenos Aires is not the most beautiful city in the world but there are some interesting things to see. If you like football, go and see Boca Juniors play. It's more like all-out war than football; certainly got my blood pumping first time."

With that the meeting was over.

"Let's get a beer and decide what we do next. I've to ring the boss and keep him updated. I'll do it from my mobile. Don't trust hotel phones on sensitive business."

Andy was delighted at George's suggestion; any reason for a beer was okay by him. They found a café and sat out on the pavement and ordered two Quilmes. If it was the largest beer in the country it must have something going for it.

"Andy," he paused, "although this sounds cut and dried my instincts are that it isn't. Millichip hasn't stayed at large all these years without a network of people looking out for him."

"But someone grassed on him."

"That's as may be. For all we know that person might be dead already. I'm just telling you we have to keep our wits about us or we'll be taken for mugs. Trust me I've done four extraditions and whilst they don't start as good as this something fouls up. I've not lost one yet and I don't plan to start now."

Andy decided there was little point in arguing. He would be outvoted and he didn't want to foul up either. "Okay what's next? I'm famished."

***

The capture of Bill Millichip had occurred the very next day after his evening with boys at the estancia. As he stepped off his Cessna in the hanger at Buenos Aries National airport they were there to greet him. He counted over 10 policemen, all armed and wearing flak jackets. He knew there was little point in resistance, most uncharacteristic for him. It must be the cancer he thought to himself. The formalities were brief. He was told in Spanish what would happen to him. He would be taken before the courts for an extradition order to be sent back to the United Kingdom. It would take at least one week.

So that was that. Years of freedom would come to an end without him extracting the revenge he so craved for. He would continue to fight whilst he had breath in his body he thought to himself. He knew in his heart he had been betrayed and he could not put it out of his mind. Not his boys surely? Perhaps the police had been closing in for some time. Perhaps the protection money was not enough. This is where the lawyers are going to earn their money. One thing for certain was he wasn't going without a fight. If he was the walking dead anyway what did he have to lose?

The journey from the airport to the police station was accompanied by the wail of sirens. Although there were no windows in the van he was travelling in he could sense a number of cars in the convoy which sped through the city and never once stopped until the police station gates were opened for their entry. To his surprise he was allowed, without having to protest, a call to his lawyer who would be there later that afternoon to see him. He was taken down a bleak set of concrete stairs to the cells below and locked up. He wasn't manhandled and almost treated with some deference. Perhaps the very policemen locking him up had enjoyed his protection money.

He dozed in his cell. He was extremely tired and in recent months had regularly slept for short periods of the day. He was awoken with the cell door being unlocked and smart man who he had never seen before walked confidently in.

"Good afternoon Mr Millichip. My name is Carlo Moyer, I am a partner in the law firm which represents you. My colleague is out of town and on his way back to see you. He will be here tomorrow or the next day and will represent you personally at your extradition hearing."

"I'm not interested in extradition hearings. For what I pay you I want out of here and now."

"I regret that will not be possible. I have seen the warrants and they deal with serious issues. It is alleged you murdered a British policeman in Peru and also shot one of your own men at a farm in England where your sister was unfortunately killed. It will take a great deal of hard work and some luck to resist these warrants."

Bill switched off. There was no point in getting angry with this man. "What happens next?"

"You have to be taken before the Court in order to be held here. That will happen tomorrow and I will be present to handle this matter. I suggest you rest. I'm told that you are unwell and I have arranged for a police doctor to examine you. This may be important in resisting extradition."

With that Carlos backed towards the door which opened and he was gone. Two policemen beckoned Bill forward and led him upstairs and along a corridor to another room. This was not a cell but had windows and a medical consulting table, various locked cabinets and a sink. He assumed this was where he might be examined. He was told to sit on the table and did so. Within minutes and old man appeared. He had a white coat so he must be the doctor. He carried out what Bill thought was a routine and cursory examination including blood pressure but asked no questions. He was about to leave without having said one word to Bill.

"Excuse me for asking but do you know why I am here?"

"You were arrested."

"Why am I here in Buenos Aires?"

"I understand you are here to see a specialist about a possible cancer."

"So what are you doing?"

"Checking that you have not been mistreated in here and that you will be fit to attend court."

"And am I?"

"Fit enough."

With that he closed his medical bag and walked out. Bill was led back to his cell for the rest of that day. He slept surprisingly well. The next morning he was given a breakfast and then handcuffed and led upstairs for his journey to Court. Carlos was present as he was loaded into the van and then the convoy raced through the city to the court building. He was ushered into a private room with dark panelling. He assumed this was the Judges chamber. He had no idea of the process; whether the hearing would be in public or not. The door opened and an elderly man walked in. He was wearing an open shirt and had no appearance of being in authority. When he spoke it was clear he was a very important person. The two policemen saluted and were instructed to bring Bill forward.

What happened next caught Bill totally by surprise. There was a commotion in the corridor and the door burst open. One of the policemen drew his gun but was shot by one of two gunmen. There was no noise. These guys were pros with silenced guns. The other policeman dropped to the floor to assist his colleague and was also shot. The judge dived behind his desk and the gunman grabbed Bill and dragged him into the corridor. Bill could see one more gunmen. He had no idea whether these men were coming after him or to save him. He just did as he was told and within a few moments his handcuffs were off and the four walked out of the court building unchallenged.

In all his life of crime this had been the first time Bill had ever been arrested. He had no idea whether his extradition could be stopped but it was irrelevant. For now he was free and able to plan the revenge he had planned for three years. Although he was glad to be free he had no idea who had arranged his escape or what they might want in return. That could wait. Life in Argentina would now be impossible. Policemen had been shot and no amount of protection money would stop them coming after him now. He would need to get out of Buenos Aires and out of Argentina for good. He would have to leave the only real, safe home he'd known; abandon it forever and still he had no idea how serious his illness was. He hated not being in control but this might have to be the pattern of his life from now on.

Chapter 6

Jamie's early life had not been deprived despite his mother's line of work. There had always been food on the table and his school uniform was never threadbare. If he wore out the knees of his trousers they were either neatly repaired or he had a new pair. He often wondered where the money had come from. It had been a shock when she had told him, but he could never bring himself to be reproachful; she had done what she had to. Jamie had never asked her for help with the bullying. He knew she would be straight round to the other boy's parents to deal with it in her way and he hadn't wanted that. Neither would he have wanted her to go to the headmaster at his school; that would be too embarrassing. In Jamie's young mind it would have probably made things worse. Only upon mature reflection might Jamie now admit doing nothing had ruined his life; so now it was payback time; but how? That was the big question.

Jamie had always lived in London. He had never travelled much. He had not wanted to go on school trips away, preferring to stay at home. He had studied hard to counter the bullying and looked set to pass all his exams. He was always near the top of his class despite hating his form teacher. His mother was so proud of him and relished reading his school reports. All seemed well until the year of his exams and his performance had dropped alarmingly. Regrettably those who noticed did nothing, so his mother had no idea.

A ferocious bout of bullying, out of school on the way home had started his decline. The bullies had been clever. They had never attacked him in public view and the beatings he took were all on his body, never his face. The bullying was continuous but that was only a contributory factor. The real cause of his slide was the night his mother had said she was terminally ill with cancer. He had gone to pieces but he was determined to show her he could cope. It would not be fair with her death sentence pending within months she should have to help him through his problems. The exams were not for another six months; he would cross that bridge when he came to it, if his mum was still alive.

That had been nearly twenty years ago. There was not a day passed he didn't think about her; had she lived, how his life might have turned out. Had he been able to attain his predicted exam results he would have then gone on to University. She had talked about it with him, told him there was enough money to fund his higher education; it was an understanding between them he would go to University. Whenever his aunt used to visit, the two sisters talked about Jamie all the time, much to his embarrassment.

It must have been in the family genes; his aunt died barely a year after his mother. Cancer had also grabbed her life and she had died quickly. Jamie grieved, not because he liked his aunt, he didn't, but because his mother had been so close to her sister. With his mother's death there was not one family member left still living in England. Her brother had left for Australia after a furious argument with Jamie's grandfather and Jamie had no idea where he was now living or what had happened to him. Jamie was alone, no relatives, no family friends and a father who had never even seen him and had no idea what had become of him. Jamie's contact with the outside world was restricted to an Internet chat line with a guy in America who seemed to have the same problems as him.

Jamie hurt all over. The beating he had taken the previous night was even more painful now than when it happened. The bruises on his body were a vivid reddish blue colour. He still had no bread, eggs or milk so he was living on black coffee, orange juice and baked beans. He knew he would have to do something to stock up the fridge. He could order from one of the big stores on the web but they all had minimum order sizes and he didn't need to stock up with much. That would be a decision for tomorrow morning. He now decided perhaps it would be safer going out in daylight and after all the years preferring the anonymity of darkness, it was a strange conclusion to come to.

He found it difficult to believe it was only twenty-four hours since this crushing experience had happened to him. It was still early evening; it was very dark outside. He could see from the one streetlight, which was flickering intermittently outside his window, the street was wet. He often turned out the lights and stood at the window watching the street below. He could not see the Convenience store from his window; it was just round the corner. His street was busy enough in daytime with some shops in the vicinity, but apart from the Convenience store they were all closed at night. His flat was a purpose built block of flats which had been modernised so it belied its fifties exterior. The warm and simple, but tastefully furnished interior was quite unlike the rest of Jamie's life; it was like a cage protecting him from the cruel world.

Jamie decided he would look at the boxes of papers he'd inherited from his mother. Quite why he had waited twenty years before opening them he was not really sure. At first after his mother's death it would have been too painful; but he had immediately opened the letter addressed to him as 'My Darling Jamie, only to be opened on my death.' The 'only' had been underlined and Jamie had decided not to disobey his mother's last wish.

It had brought him immediately to tears and he had found at the tender age of sixteen it was difficult to understand the will and the financial arrangements she had made for him. Having accepted he was not going to live with her sister, she had told him to live in their flat for two years until he was eighteen and ready for University. She had paid the landlord two years rent in advance. Jamie thought that strange but never dwelt on it; perhaps it was her way of keeping him focussed on his education. There was nothing he had to do except get a death certificate and deal with the Funeral Director who had also been sent all the relevant information. There had been a large parcel, which contained over £100,000 in used £5 and £10 notes. He had been astonished to see it; he stared at the bundles of money. His mind could not really comprehend what his Mother had done to keep them together, but neither could he condemn her. £100,000 was a hell of a lot. Now at thirty-five years of age he permitted himself a wry smile and thought 'She must have been very good at it'.

Jamie had never had girlfriends; a few one night stands but after what his mother had said to him that night sitting on his bed, he had decided never to resort to sex with a prostitute. Her decision had been forced on her when his father had abandoned her. He refused to think she had been a stripper or 'call girl' before she had fallen pregnant, although it was a question he had never put to her, possibly fearful of the answer. He put further conjecture out of his mind. He didn't want to know the answer; whatever it was.

The letter had been specific about how he was to invest the money; she had opened accounts in his name with lots of banks and building societies.

What surprised him in retrospect was the ease with which all this happened. Rarely did he have to answer any questions as to why a young man might be wishing to deposit large amounts of cash. Her last letter had been about five pages; it gave him all the guidance a parent would have given a teenager as he grew into adulthood. Jamie still had the letter. He had read and re-read it so many times it was in danger of falling apart. Whenever he held it in his hands he had a strange feeling she was still there watching over him. In the event that Jamie would ever get married and have kids, which was highly unlikely, he hoped he would be as good a parent as she had been.

This night he felt the need to be close to her again. He opened the two boxes of papers and photographs he had collected from a cupboard when on his eighteenth birthday he had finally moved out of their flat. He had done everything exactly as his mother had ordained.

His hands were trembling as he peeled away the gummed tape she had sealed them with all those years ago. The first box contained two photograph albums. He opened one to see pictures of his mother, his aunt and the uncle he had never known. There were photos of his grandparents and he found it strangely comforting to know at some stage of his early life he had been within a normal family. There were shots of family holidays by the sea, always in England. It seems the family finances had never extended to holidays abroad.

The second album included photos of his mother with friends she had made later in life after she had left home. In many, but not all, there was a man. It was obvious the two were close. They were always cuddling or holding hands and the photographs appeared to cover periods of more than one year. Jamie wondered the significance of this man. He took a few of the photos out of their clips and turned them over. His name was Frank and many were taken at the Kentish seaside around Margate. The dates were all just before he was born; he wondered could this be his father?

This stirred in him a curiosity he had never felt before.

Chapter 7

The visit in daylight the next day to the Convenience store was uneventful. Jamie stocked up on a lot more than the milk, bread and eggs he had needed. He had provisions and ready meals, long-life milk and bread to freeze enough to delay his next shopping trip.

It was a strange thing. Even the check-out operator remarked on it. "You having a party?" she had quipped.

Jamie just ignored the question and paid the girl. He loaded his purchases into two carrier bags and walked out of the store.

"Misery," she had said as he turned to leave. He heard but decided against responding and headed home.

Quite why he had stocked up he really didn't know; but if it put off the next trouble for a while, that had to be good. He decided it was safer shopping by day but he still didn't want to be out on the streets more than necessary.

He had been forming in his mind why he felt the need to fight back. To do so invited even more trouble and he'd seen more than enough to last a lifetime; and he was only thirty-six. Maybe it was this last attack, particularly vicious; worse by far than any beating he had ever endured in his painful life. Maybe it was because he'd gone to help somebody else and had been punished for it. His thoughts were not rational. Most of his life it was purely humiliation he'd suffered. He had been in a few fights and some were probably a result of his own short fuse. He had got the first punch in but had usually been on the wrong end of a thrashing, but nothing like he had endured this week.

'No,' he thought, 'this time I'm really going to get my own back and sod the consequences.' If it went bad for him so be it. He had been near to suicide on a couple of occasions in his life and the thought of death didn't frighten him. Pain bothered him and he'd been subjected to so much pain it was time someone else should know the feeling. Although his pain had been physical on many occasions, more usually it was mental pain. He believed from what he had read on the web he was, almost certainly, a psychological case and if ever he was seriously examined by doctors they would in hindsight class him as a 'head case waiting to explode'. Well, perhaps that time was now.

He turned on his computer to see what he could ascertain about 'revenge'. His searches led him to 'Wikipedia', which he used for most things that needed explanation and the site led him to 'murderers'. Quite why he should do so was not clear to him, but he clicked on the word.

Jamie was fascinated by what he read. He clicked on 'favourites' to save the site and decided he would go back in a little later and look in depth at this fascinating topic. Why he was so fascinated he wasn't sure; after all he had tried to keep out of people's way as much as he could.

It was a cold blustery day outside. He didn't want to go out but he felt the fresh air and a walk would stretch his muscles, which were taught and strained after his beating. He grabbed his jacket and opened his door and went down to the street lobby. He paused wondering whether this was a good idea. It was the first time he had been out other than to the store for some months. He hadn't worked now for almost a year. Would it be tempting fate, inviting some other humiliation upon him? He nearly turned back but something made him go through the door and out into the street. He hadn't even looked up or down the street to see if there were threats lurking. He turned towards the park, which was about half a mile away. The park in daytime was relatively safe with mums and their toddlers so Jamie thought he should be okay.

He found walking difficult; he could not straighten his back so he was hunched forward but he found the fresh air invigorating. It was a long time since he had felt so in charge of a simple thing like being outside. It was his own choice to go out late at night so fewer people would see him. It now dawned on him perhaps that had not been such a bright idea; maybe being out in daylight was the lesser of two evils.

His self-imposed isolation had started the previous year. It was after he had left his last job. His boss had been a bully and it had brought Jamie to the verge of a nervous breakdown. He had in his depression, even considered suicide; but something about the cosy, safe nature of living in his flat made life at least bearable. He had enough money not to need to look for another job for a reasonable period. He wanted to get his life back in order and then decide what to do next. He had gone round to the local pub but the landlord was a nasty type who took great delight in ignoring Jamie and refusing to serve him. The last straw had been when he asked Jamie for some identification to prove he was old enough to buy a drink. This in itself was just a cruel humiliation he could have lived with but it was done with a bar full of people. It had led him to stop going to pubs altogether.

Jamie had become a recluse from that moment on. Now was the time to fight back; but how, he had yet to figure out.

***

Jamie sat before his computer screen; he had keyed into his 'favourites' and brought up a number of files on revenge. He was comforted at the descriptions of revenge as 'primarily retaliation against a person or group in response to a perceived wrongdoing'.

Rather than justice he was taken with the notion that revenge usually had a more injurious role than harmonious intention, usually consisting of forcing the wrongdoer to suffer the same pain as was originally inflicted.

Jamie considered this for quite some time. If he wanted to get even it wasn't enough to bully those who bullied him. Jamie sat staring at the screen thinking. How could he get revenge? How could he do it in a way that the victim would know it was Jamie; know why it was happening and suffer in that one moment for all the pain Jamie had suffered?

He was mesmerised looking at the word 'revenge'. He could not be more certain than he was at this moment; he was now going to take control over his life. "I've accepted this crap for too long," he muttered to himself almost willing the computer to start a conversation with him. The difficulty was how. How could he change twenty years of being dumped on? He reached for a scrap of paper. He was going to think this through properly; consider all the options.

He made himself a cup of coffee and sat back in front of the computer screen. He wrote 'revenge' at the top of the page:

> *"For who – me or all people who suffer as I do?*
>
> *Against whom - a perfect stranger or somebody I know?"*

He thought about these two headings for a while. He was so absorbed his coffee had gone cold, then he wrote in big bold capital letters; 'FOR ME … AND SOMEBODY I KNOW'. So that was it. He would have to hurt somebody he knew in a way that they knew it was him - and the reason why.

He started a list. This could be a very long list he thought, but when it came to writing a name it was somehow more difficult. For a minute he couldn't identify any name; whom did he hate most? Was it to be someone or thing from the here and now, something that had just happened or from some time in his early life. Both presented problems. If it were to be the thugs who had beaten him just a couple of days ago; that would be difficult. There were more of them and if he hit back they would be around to make his life a continuing misery. What if he was to single one out; he might need to do it in a way so he didn't know it was Jamie who had done it? That seemed to defeat the object and what if he was unsuccessful? Tackling any thug had its dangers; they would be used to someone fighting back and that would lead to more trouble for him. This seemed a dangerous route to take. If he were to choose anybody from his early life how would he trace him? He decided this needed a lot more thought; revenge had to be certain and above all, sweet.

He continued staring at the sheet of paper. So far all he had decided was he wanted revenge, for him and he wanted the person to know it was him and why. He started writing names of people who had bullied him at school. He realised that was leading nowhere. It would be impossible to find them. He thought about who had hurt him the most in his life. Then it dawned on him; it wasn't a person who had hurt him by being there. It was somebody whose absence had really affected his life, his absent father. He wrote the word 'Father' in bold letters on his pad and ringed it several times until the repetition scored the paper so it separated from the rest of the page. He took the torn paper and pinned it to the small notice board by his computer; he was pretty certain he now knew the solution to his problem.

For now all he could be certain of was he had to find out exactly the identity of his father; was it Frank who had appeared in so many of the photos his mother had kept? If it was, and it was crucial to be certain, what type of man could have deserted his mother when she became pregnant? He knew this was not unique; he didn't care whether it was or not. It had defined his life; made him what he was by not being there for him and by some process or other he was going to make him pay; how, he had no idea. He sat there in front of the screen watching the screen saver scrolling up, down and sideways. The screensaver annoyed him.

"You are history," he said to the screen as he brought up a file of alternatives. He scrolled down the list and none grabbed him. He logged onto PowerPoint and started to design a new screensaver. It only took him a few moments. It was almost all black; the colour of death and in the most obscure font he could find, Matisse ITC, he typed the word 'REVENGE' in caps. He put the word into brilliant red and drew blood dripping from it. He liked the effect and set it as his new screensaver.

This was a start; maybe only a small step but it was action at last.

He thought about the walk in the park and how invigorated he had felt; he wanted to enjoy the feeling again. He had denied himself this simple pleasure for too long, but it was important nothing should get in his way and spoil this newfound simple pleasure, taken for granted and enjoyed by everyone else. He had nothing he could take as a weapon to defend himself. He had never carried a knife and if he were stopped by a policeman that would mean trouble. He started rummaging through his odds and sods drawer and found the next best thing. He had a big 'Maglite' torch. It was metal cased and with the batteries it was solid and heavy; it would hurt someone if he hit them. A suitable weapon, he thought; there should be no law about carrying a torch, even in broad daylight.

It was a cold day, even for the first week of March; a bitter wind forced Jamie to wrap up with two fleeces and a scarf and ski hat. He had always resisted a hood; he hated the 'hoodie' thug culture. It was not as enjoyable as his walk the day before. He decided to walk quickly to keep warm and he kept the torch in his hand ready to use it if need be. With every stride he felt more and more confident being outside. Why, oh why, had he denied himself the daylight all these years? It was like being reborn; new sensations re-entered his thoughts; memories of his early childhood before the regime of bullying had forced him into his reclusive shell.

He walked past a shop with a gang of boys standing in the doorway. All too often in the past, he would have turned round or crossed the road to avoid confrontation. Possibly this had provoked attention of those who otherwise would have paid him no heed. He half hesitated but then decided he would walk into the shop just to see what might happen. Was this a good idea or just plain reckless? He was committed now. He had not broken his stride and he was up to them. He brushed past a smaller lad leaning on the shop window nearest the door and into the tobacconist shop. He had no idea what he wanted so he bought chewing gum. He paid the shopkeeper; the affable Asian smiled, offered Jamie his change with thanks and gestured towards the door.

"Bloody kids; always in my doorway. I don't know how many customers are avoiding me because they hang outside but takings are right down. The police do nothing. I keep onto them but they ignore me."

Jamie grunted his thanks and took his change. He was not yet up to making social chit chat at this time. As he opened the door, there they all were, but to his surprise they were not interested in him but neither were they getting out of his way. He pushed past and nobody bothered and he was away into the street. It was only at this time he realised that his knuckles hurt. His grip on his torch had made his hand ache. He was both encouraged and relieved this outing had gone so well. It was now time to return to his sanctuary to carry out more planning.

Jamie opened the door of the flat and went in to the cosy, safe environment. "That's enough for one day."

He made himself a sandwich and a cup of tea. He sat at his favourite seat with a view to the street below. He was feeling quite proud of himself; but he must not rush into his plan for revenge. He got out his mother's boxes again. He was confident that Frank in the photos could be his father but then in his mother's line of work so could plenty of others. He would need to be more certain than this. Unfortunately there was no family resemblance between him and this man Frank. His mother knew who Jamie's father was. Had she destroyed all evidence of him or was it Frank who regularly appeared in the photos?

The other box had lots of papers. He was looking for a birth certificate, anything that would seal it for him. He found a birth certificate envelope. On the outside in his mother's hand was written 'My birth certificate'. He opened the envelope and there was the certificate for his mother, Caroline McLeish. He read the document carefully and felt a tinge of sadness. Everyone listed on that certificate was dead. He did not know the definition of being an orphan but since his mother's death he always considered himself to be one; no father and a mother snatched from him by cancer. He could not clearly remember his grandparents; he had met them on a few occasions.

He was about to return the certificate into the envelope but he felt something else inside the envelope. He extracted another piece of folded paper. It was his birth certificate; this was it. This was the point at which all would become clear. It was carefully folded and appeared not to have been handled very often; not like his mother's that had various rubber stamps on the back where it had been used for official purposes.

He carefully unfolded it in anticipation of finding the truth at last. To his disappointment against the name of the father was written the words 'not known'. He stared at this official document designed to be the absolute proof of who you are and where you came from. All sorts of different thoughts were flooding into his mind.

It made him angry to find nothing conclusive. For a moment he blamed his mother, but he immediately regretted the notion. He folded the certificates and put the envelope to one side. He picked up the photo of the man he was building up to be his father. The date on the back tallied; it was the year before he was born but it gave no month. It was definitely a summer picture and he had been born at the beginning of May. He rummaged through some more papers. There were lots of letters. His mother had preferred writing to using the phone and there was a bundle of letters to her sister. They were tied with a silk ribbon. He untied the knot and spread them on the coffee table. They were in date order so he started with the most recent. He wished he hadn't. He wished now his curiosity had not got the better of him. He should have left things as they were. Perhaps in this case ignorance was bliss.

He was staring at what he was certain was his mother's last ever letter. The writing was spidery; it must have been a real struggle for her and Jamie could not remember posting it for her. Her last days had been in a hospice. His aunt had arranged it all for him. She must have put these letters away for Jamie to have.

Jamie had difficulty with the writing:

'My dearest Susie

I am at peace and I can barely find the strength to write. Life was never fair but I have never regretted the life I led. Jamie was the only good thing, my precious Jamie who bravely battles against life without complaint. I know he hurts but he has never complained to me. At first I thought of wading in for him but when it was at its worst I had no strength for him. Darling Jamie what will become of him? He is so young.

Look out for him, he has money and the rent on the flat is paid up for two years.

It is so sad that he will never have a father; Frank would have been so proud of his work at school. He will be the first in the family to go to University. I so wish I could be there to see him. Although Frank wanted no part of us I always kept tabs on him. He ended up with six menswear shops but he had to sell them. I asked one of my old friends to see if Frank still had his original shop in Marylebone High Street. She told me it looks a bit run down but it is still a tailor and menswear shop.

I shall have to close now; I have no strength to sit up. I hope you can read my writing.

I love you and brother Jim, wherever he may be. God Bless.

All my love,

Carol'

Now he could barely make out the words; the tears were streaming, blurring his mother's spidery handwriting. Jamie reached for his handkerchief. He hadn't felt so emotional, since that day when he thought his world would end; the day his mother told him she was going to die. He put the letter down. He wanted time to contemplate. He lay on his bed. This was not the moment to advance his plan for revenge; but now he had a name and a thirty six year old photograph. He felt emotionally drained as he stared at the ceiling and within a short time he fell asleep.

Chapter 8

Sam got the kids ready after breakfast. She was looking forward to her meeting with George Strachan and lunch. Since she had left the force it had been a regular feature of her life, which she cherished. She did not regret leaving the police, how could she with Eddie and three lovely kids to look after. It was the link back to her father and she enjoyed meeting Juan Ramos when he was around.

She set off for her mother's, which was about a fifteen-minute drive. She loved looking after the children. Sam had been an only child so this was her opportunity to indulge herself and her grandchildren. Sam was cutting it a bit fine for time so she dropped them off with no time for a chat. She needed to catch a train and as she parked the car she could see it was just pulling in the station. Fortunately she was able to buy a ticket from the automatic machine and she jumped on as the doors were closing. She was out of breath and promised to leave herself more time in future.

She arrived at the reception of New Scotland Yard. She was always impressed and somewhat humbled there was a pre-written pass for her; it saved so much time. Within minutes, George appeared and took her upstairs to the squad room. This was where George worked; it was similar to the facilities she had known in the Drug Squad office. She followed George into his glass sided cubicle and sat down while he went to get coffees. There was a ritual for these monthly 'get-togethers' which was very comforting to Sam, almost as though she was still part of the force, but without the hassle. George returned and sat down at his desk.

"Well Sam, what's been happening to you since I last saw you?"

"Nothing of note. All is well with my lump. I told you I think it's a boy. I don't mind but I think Eddie would like another boy. He says two of each would be good but not twins again."

"Is that likely?"

"No, thank God."

"I'm on a tight schedule today. I'm okay for lunch but we'll have to be a bit quicker. I only found out after you left home that I've got to attend a meeting but I've some news for you, but I'm not sure you're going to want to hear it."

"Sounds like you feel I need to; let's have it."

"Juan Ramos came in to see me yesterday. It appears things are happening in Peru. He has heard that there has been a big crackdown by the new police chief. He was a family friend of Juan's father and he has been brought out of semi-retirement to shake out the bad guys; he's been pretty effective from what Juan tells me.

After the shooting when you were held captive all sorts of changes were made; the simplest was a rotation of partners quite regularly. The good guys never wanted to be paired off with a crooked copper and there was a lot of fall out as people reported others. When Juan was seconded to us it was partly for his own safety. He had many enemies amongst those who feared the truth. He has been most useful here in London and he has identified a number of known traffickers we weren't aware of."

"But what is it I don't want to hear?"

"I'm coming to that. When I told you Bill had escaped I didn't have all the details. The official report was received last night. Our guys weren't actually there when Bill escaped in Buenos Aires. They had the extradition papers and he had been escorted to the Judge's chambers at the Court for a special hearing in front of the judge. Actually at the Judge's chambers at the Court three gunmen shot the two policemen guarding Millichip and threatened to shoot the judge. They got clean away. Our guys had no idea for at least half an hour. They say that Bill must have had some Argentine police assistance. The family remains well-connected out there…"

Sam interjected, "This man seems to lead a charmed life. When will he be finally caught?"

She felt strangely tearful. She had been building up in her mind he was now out of their lives and once again he was right back, not quite centre stage but a real liability.

"I know. It's disappointing for you and it makes us look fools as well. We'll get him in the end."

"I hope so and not before I'm too old to care, please."

"More bad news, I'm afraid. Juan's friend on the Argentine force says Bill may already have left Argentina but where to we have no idea. He can't go back to his Estancia. The authorities have declared him public enemy numero uno."

"George what do we know?" This lack of action was irritating Sam, quite why she wasn't sure. It had been hanging around for nearly four years now and she had got used to the idea. Somehow it was different now. The medal photos and the interview had all brought it sharply back; and she was due to deliver. Maybe that was the reason.

"If he's left Argentina we have to consider the possibility he may come back to settle old scores. We know how violent he became and I wouldn't be surprised if he plans revenge on those who he feels were responsible for his sister's death."

"But he was there when Julia was shot and he shot the man who killed her."

"There's more to it. Juan thinks he plans to come after you. Sam, I haven't told you till now but we have been keeping a watch on your house. Nothing overt but we feel you, Eddie and the kids could be in danger."

"Whether we are or not, I'm not going to be a prisoner in my own home." Sam could again feel anger building up inside her again.

"Hold on Sam, don't go getting all stewed up. This is a warning you and we have to be vigilant. Bill is dangerous. He thinks he's well connected but the word is his former associates don't want him near them. It's crucial we are all vigilant until we can locate Bill; we have Spanish, Argentinean, Peruvian and our own warrants out for him so there are a lot of resources out there looking for him."

"I need to talk this through with Eddie before I agree to anything." She had calmed a little. "I'm sorry if I was sharp but you know Bill is still a raw nerve with me. I agree with Juan and still think he might do something to us if he could, but permanent police protection is a little over the top don't you think?"

"No, I don't actually. Sam you mean a lot to the police force and everything to me. Medals don't get handed out for nothing and we, and I mean the hierarchy would be greatly upset if something happened to you we could have prevented. You know what you mean to me so I take this responsibility personally. So for the moment whatever we have been doing will continue and if you hadn't clocked it well it can't be that intrusive, can it?"

"There is no answer to that is there? Okay then, but when I have talked to Eddie I'll get back to you."

Let's go and have a bite of lunch. Today it is in-house. I can't spare the time to go out."

"Why don't we get a sandwich and continue chatting here?"

"Okay, if you don't mind that would be great for me. I'll make it up to you next time."

They continued chatting whilst one of George's team went for a sandwich for them. Sam was disturbed by what George had told her. The more she thought about it the more logical it was her family should have some protection. It had only been her stubbornness that prevented her accepting it earlier. She suspected George knew as well. He was such a good friend; he was a perfect replacement for her late father.

She thought about George. He had been away from duty for a long period before he was well enough to return to duty. His leg had been shattered by two bullets in the hail of fire as the gunmen tried to shoot their way out. Her father had been shot just as he had got George to safety behind a car. At the post mortem the pathologist had dug two more bullets from her father's body, hit whilst he was dragging George to safety.

She knew from George's wife that he relives the day in frequent nightmares as he saw his partner selflessly give his life for him. He had been a regular visitor to Sam when she was growing up with her mother. Then all of a sudden he had stopped coming and there was only the occasional phone call. Sam had found that strange. She had never asked him about it and she had no idea why at this point it seemed important to know.

"Changing the subject somewhat; I always meant to ask why you stopped visiting a year after dad's death."

George looked startled at the question out of the blue.

"Your mother told me she felt I was in no way responsible for his death but she wanted to get on with the rest of her life. She told me she had no intention of remarrying and she wanted her life to be as normal as possible. She said my kindnesses to you both were lovely but delaying closure for her. I was a bit hurt at the time but she was right; life goes on and it was delaying that moment."

"I wish mum had told me she had asked you to stop visiting. I think I would have preferred to know and I would have understood."

"Water under the bridge now, Sam. Forget about it. I speak to your mother more often now and we have a great relationship. I'm not sure I should tell you this, but you probably guessed she asked me to keep an eye on you whilst you worked here; it was easier said than done. I asked the boss whether I could tell her you'd gone to Peru but it was strictly forbidden."

"Probably for the best, especially in view of what happened."

Sam was startled by a knock on the glass partition. There was Juan Ramos, smiling at her. George beckoned him to come in.

"Oh Juan, it's so good to see you."

"And to see you, and looking so plump. When is it due?"

"Plump, I'm seven months." She said indignantly as she hugged him. "You haven't changed a bit. Still got the same leather jacket, I see."

"Lucky jacket. Maybe not me changing, but you, yes. And life with Bill on the loose, you must be careful."

"Don't you start."

"Seriously, I am told he is now even more dangerous man. You do what Mr Strachan says. Promise me. Promise me Sam."

"Okay, okay. Leave it there for now. Now whilst I have you both here I want to invite you both to a party, well a lunch party."

"What are we celebrating?" George enquired.

"Well having just got the photos of the award ceremony we never did celebrate it at the time. George, I want you and your wife, Juan, mum and Vince at our house for a Sunday lunch. Don't plan on driving afterwards. We can put you up now the extension has been completed. I've just got to clear the date with mum. I was in such a rush this morning I forgot. It is the last Sunday in March but I will confirm it."

"I'll be there," Juan said smiling.

I'll check with Jane and I'll get her to ring you Sam. It will be great to see Vince, I haven't seen him for such a long time."

That's settled then, let's says it's definite unless I ring tonight."

With that Juan made a move to leave. Sam kissed him goodbye on both cheeks.

"Sam, will you speak to Eddie tonight about Bill. I need to set things up. Get him to ring my mobile if he has anything he wants to ask me, anything at all. You will be sure to do it, please."

"Yes George, I'll speak to him," Sam wanted to sound irritated but smiled and gathered her things. She was earlier than she had expected so this was a rare moment of luxury. Time for shopping.

She arrived at the station near her mother's house laden with bags of clothes for the baby and drove to pick up the kids. She wondered whether to tell her about the conversation with George and Juan but decided against it until she had spoken to Eddie. She gathered up the kids and strapped them in the seats and prepared to leave.

"I nearly forgot. We are having a lunch party at the end of the month. George and his wife will be there and Vince. I'll ring with the date tonight. Stay over."

"What's this in aid of?"

Sam wondered whether to say the real reason in case she decided not to come. "Just a gathering of friends before I get too fat and lazy to do it."

"OK, my diary's not full," she joked, "but let me know so I don't accept another date. I've so many men friends these days it..." she let the joke trail off; it didn't seem funny.

Sam arrived home and Eddie was sitting reading the paper. The girls ran to him and he sat one on each knee. Mark was asleep in Sam's arms.

"You're home early, what's up?"

"Nothing, just thought I'd come home and maybe we could get some clothes for the baby."

"Too late, can you unload the car for me and when you've finished I need to talk to you?"

"Sounds ominous," as he went out to the car.

Eddie returned and smiled. "See what you mean," as he dumped the bags on the floor, "so what do you need to talk to me about."

"Two things. The lunch is on but I forgot the date so I have to ring and confirm and Bill Millichip escaped in Buenos Aires and George thinks he may be heading back in England."

"So what?"

"George wants a protection squad for us. Juan says his contacts say he has comeback to settle scores with the gang and us," she said in a matter-of-fact way.

"Yes, I know."

"What do you mean you know," Sam was upset, "have they told you already?" This was her domain and she was indignant he knew before her.

"Hold on darling. George hasn't told me anything. I spotted a car parked in roughly the same position each day and I was about to ask what he was doing there and he showed me his warrant card and explained."

"Explained what?"

"That they were taking precautions because they feared Bill Millichip might come back but had no concrete evidence."

"Why didn't you say something?"

"Didn't want to worry you."

"Well, they want to ramp it up now he's escaped."

"Good, makes sense."

"I thought you wouldn't want it."

"Look, what I want and what's best for the family are quite different things."

"OK, I'll get back to George and say it's OK."

"So let's get onto really important things; what have you bought?"

Chapter 9

Jamie had been in turmoil since the day he had read his mother's final letter. So now he knew the identity of his father; something he never bothered himself with since he was young and told he had deserted them. It was a strange feeling. He was both upset and exhilarated; upset because it was an invasion on his private life; exhilarated, he now had something tangible for his revenge. The fact it was his father who he had blamed all these years for the unfairness to his mother and to himself would make it all the sweeter.

"Hold on," he said out loud to himself, "what if I can't find him and what sort of revenge can I exact? Do I want to hurt him, like he's hurt me; or do I want to humiliate him for what he did to mum?"

He sat at his computer and the graphic 'Revenge' stared at him, transfixing him. What was the point of humiliation; that was what he suffered every time he had gone out over the recent months? He needed revenge. He clicked on the Google icon and up came the favourites list. He had created a whole folder of sites relating to revenge and he scrolled down. He was undecided which to click on and he came to a decision. What was the point of deciding on a course of action if he couldn't find his victim? First things first, who was Frank and where could he find him?

He reopened his mother's letter and decided the first thing was a walk down Marylebone High Street to see what menswear shops would be there. The High Street was a busy north-south cut through from the main Marylebone High Road running west to east across the city to Oxford Street near Bond Street underground. He identified on Google where he had to head for and with his newfound thirst for getting out and confronting his demons he decided to go that morning. It was a bright morning so what better time. He grabbed his coat and his protector, the 'maglite' torch, strode along the street heading for the Underground which would take him to Warren Street station and he would walk from there. He was again surprised at how little he feared walking in broad daylight and he relished the experience. Who knows, he thought, he might even get a suntan this year. As he reached the Underground his confidence waned. The claustrophobic atmosphere of the escalators and the narrow platforms made him feel edgy. As the train approached, preceded by a wind so strong the lady next to him almost lost her hat, he started to relax. This was short-lived as the train, which was not particularly full, offered him no chance of escape if trouble started.

He tried to rationalise why he was scared, why his hands were damp with sweat? Was it the three youths in hoodies sat with their feet on the opposite seats? Were they a threat? They appeared disinterested in him. He looked through to the next carriage and could see a British Transport policeman travelling on the tube and he decided at the next stop to move into that carriage. The train rattled into the station and screeched to a halt. He exited the carriage and was dismayed to see the policeman also got off the train. What should he do; move carriages as planned or stay where he was? He hopped back as he was; maybe the occupants were unlikely to bother him. His breathing calmed as he got himself together. What could be the problem? There were at least twenty other passengers. He counted twelve more stations to go and as the line got closer to the centre of the City it was sure to get busier. Nevertheless it was a struggle to keep control. He was relieved to get out at Warren Street and head towards the fresh air and light.

He stood on the pavement outside the station wondering which way to go and was jostled by other passengers entering and leaving the station. He saw a map on the station wall and discovered he was on the right side of the busy Marylebone High Road and he walked along to Marylebone High Street. It was sharp contrast to the main Marylebone Road, probably the main arteries for traffic passing across central London.

By contrast it was more like a village atmosphere with a small shops and cafes with accommodation above. He walked down the road looking both sides for a menswear shop. It hadn't taken long and on the left hand side there it was, a tailors and menswear shop. The sign gave no clue as to who owned it and at this stage he had no intention of going inside. This was the earliest stage of his, as yet, hazy plan. He walked the entire length until the road split before crossing Wigmore Street; to the left it became Marylebone Lane, which was very narrow and straight on it was Thayer Street. He retraced his steps and stood diagonally across from the shop on the other side of the road contemplating his next move. It was twelve thirty and he sat at a pavement café looking at the shop front. It looked dowdy; his mother's letter had said it had once been a thriving business but it certainly wasn't now. He ordered a coffee and sat for at least half an hour and not one customer went in; very few even looked in the window. It was not an inviting display.

The waiter was staring at Jamie wondering just how long he could make one coffee last. There was now much more activity as office workers were taking their lunch break and a queue had formed outside a sandwich bar opposite. There were now no tables free in the café and Jamie was just about to get up when a man walked out of the tailors and locked the door. He strode purposely and went into the sandwich bar, ignoring the queue. Within a minute he was out again and walked back to the shop clutching a package; he unlocked the door and went in, locking it behind him. The man looked in his early sixties but it was impossible for Jamie to positively identify him from that short sighting, but at last he knew he was making progress. The waiter hovered with the bill and was surprised when Jamie left the change. The waiter beamed; he had not expected a tip, he had marked Jamie as a definite no.

"Thanks, have a nice day."

Jamie thought it sounded as though he didn't mean it but smiled back.

"Do you know who runs that tailors over there?" He had no idea why he asked or why the waiter should know.

"No idea but the sandwich shop should know. He goes there every day except Wednesday."

"Why not Wednesday?"

"He closes half day."

"OK thanks." He walked off hoping not to have aroused suspicions about his question. This was enough for one day; he was beginning to feel nervous about being out. He walked back to the station and headed for the sanctuary of his flat. He sat down looking out at the street below, the earlier sunshine had given way to a dull cloudy afternoon with rain threatening. So what did he know? More correctly, what did he think he knew? Yes, there was a tailor in Marylebone High Street; yes, it was the only one and the owner was about the right age. He needed to find out whether it was indeed Frank.

Jamie decided this was enough excitement for one day and he was surprised how tired he was. By any normal person's working day he had done nothing but commute to London, walk down a street or two and had a cup of coffee, but by his standards of recent years this was a very full day. He turned on the TV to see what was on and trawled through the endless channels offered by SKY and settled on an old gangster movie with hard man James Cagney. He wasn't really watching it but it relaxed him, despite the constant rattle of gunfire as rival mobsters battled it out. He never saw the end; he was asleep and woke to SKY News reporting 'breaking news' on the murder of an elderly man in broad daylight in a street not far from his flat. Although it had happened earlier and there must have been considerable noise of police sirens he had heard nothing.

He sat at his computer with the sound of a reporter droning on and interviewing a passer-by who had seen the murder take place but for a reason, which wasn't clear had done nothing about it and had no idea what the murderer looked like. It sounded familiar, nobody cares enough to do anything; he stared at computer screen with the word 'revenge' staring back at him.

He needed to make progress and could have done so already if he had plucked up courage to ask in the sandwich shop to see if he could identify whether the owner had been his father. He wondered whether he should actually go into the shop and strike up a conversation and see what transpired, but he did not feel confident enough, or was it brave enough, to do so. He would have to find that courage and soon. It was important not to quit now. He had gained a small measure of control over his life and he wanted more. This was not a daydream; just to find out and then go back to being a recluse; this was to be his springboard to a real life. So the priority for the next few days was for Jamie to find out whether the man he had seen coming from the shop was Frank, what was his surname and was he his father?

***

Sam was sitting at the breakfast bar drinking coffee watching news of a murder that had happened in Tooting that afternoon. She was surprised there was so much coverage, it had only happened a few hours before. She wondered idly how busy the Murder squad room would be and who would be assigned to the case; would it be anybody she knew? So much happens and so fast in the Met. Her weekly calls with George Strachan were pretty routine, more about mutual friends and family and other than Bill Millichip they talked 'business' less and less. She was daydreaming when the phone rang; it startled her and she immediately picked it up so the loud ringing would not wake Mark. The twins were at her mother's and she would need to go soon to collect them, unless Eddie offered to do it. What a blessing that would be, she thought.

"Hello," she said briefly unable to think of her own phone number.

"Hi darling, you sound miles away, you okay?"

"Yes fine, daydreaming about you, as always."

"I'm leaving early; do you want me to go to your mum's to collect the kids?"

"That would be brilliant, you must be a mind reader."

"What?"

"Oh nothing, just thinking aloud."

"We need to celebrate; I've secured a valuable contract. It's a pity you can't have a drink."

"I'll make something special for dinner. One little glass should be okay; I'll put a bottle in the fridge. See you later."

Mark began to cry in his cot. It never ceased to amaze her whenever Eddie was on the phone or about to arrive home he seemed to sense his presence. The phone rang again.

"What have you forgotten?" she said without thinking.

"As far as I know nothing. What sort of question is that to open up with?" It was George Strachan.

"I was just speaking to Eddie and thought he'd forgotten something. Sorry George, what can I do for you?"

"I have to cancel our lunch this week. I've just been handed a murder enquiry in Tooting. It's going to keep me busy for a while."

"I was just watching it on the news and wondered who it was talking to the press; I didn't recognise him."

"Well, he's new and the powers that be want a more experienced set of hands running this one and that's me."

"Congratulations, I think. Okay just ring when you have time."

"I'm hoping this will be quick. Give my love to the kids. Bye."

Sam put the phone down and gathered Mark into her arms. "Daddy will be home soon." He giggled happily.

Chapter 10

Jamie had never had the luxury of friends he could talk to. His was a lonely world. Even at school he was a loner, beaten by bullies, always wanting to be in the background. He had been shunned by the girl he fancied in his class. Girls at that age had the upper hand and always played hard to get but she had just told him to go away; not nasty, but it left little room for encouragement to try again. After his mum had died there had been no contact with classmates; even one boy who'd also been bullied shunned him.

He was reading the Sunday newspaper supplement when an item caught his eye. It was an interview with Ruth Danson-Whyte. She was working within the Metropolitan Police on studies of violence to children within families. She had written three novels about characters drawn from the dregs of life, all of whom appeared to have come from secure families but had left home as a result of violence. The last book had become a best seller and negotiations were progressing the film rights. The article explained her background and this sparked Jamie's interest. The photograph looked vaguely familiar but he couldn't think why.

He could not put the picture of the woman out of his mind. Why was it familiar? He puzzled for a while and then was about to switch on the computer when it hit him. In his early twenties he had a casual relationship with a woman. He had befriended her in a pub. He never found out her name. It might have been Ruth, then again it could have been any other name. She had lived in a squat and looked dirty. She said she had come from a good family but had left after the death of her father and continuous rows with her mother. She had run off with a guitarist who turned into an addict and had started living rough. She moved in with his mates in an empty house, which was not quite derelict, but within an ace of becoming so.

They had chatted at the bar and both were quite drunk. He said he was going for a take away and she had agreed to join him provided he paid. They had stopped for a Kentucky Fried Chicken and ate it sitting on a bench in the park near his flat. She was easy to talk to and Jamie enjoyed talking with her. He had no ideas about getting involved; he was starved of conversation with anybody so it was such a change to his routine.

"I suppose you expect a shag now?" the girl had blurted out.

Jamie was totally floored. He had no idea what to say but the prospect of getting laid for the first time in his life made his decision easy. It had started to rain.

"Sounds good to me," he said as his loins started to engage. He did not want her back to his flat, "Where, your place?"

"Depends whether anyone's in, if the lights on we'll have to find somewhere else."

They walked about a quarter of a mile with his erection straining against his zip. He was desperate for a pee. He went behind a bush and she followed him in and squatted. The urge to have sex meant he would do anything and he didn't want to louse it up. They reach the house. The light was on.

"We'll have to do out here."

"What standing up?"

With that she leaned against the doorway and lifted her skirt. Jamie had not expected this. He had never had it lying down so standing up was going to be tricky. She was much taller than him and he would need to stand on something just to reach her. This was all going wrong and he toyed with asking her to come home with him.

"What's the matter, don't you want it?"

"Yes, but not like this."

"How then? We can't shag on the grass it's pissing down." Then the penny dropped. "Okay. You stand on the door step and then we'll be okay."

Jamie put his hand between her thighs to take her knickers down but she had none on. He started to panic. Standing there in a doorway seemed so unreal. What if someone came by? Things were out of his control and she undid his belt and she pulled down his zip. He felt stupid as first his trousers and then his pants fell to his ankles.

She pulled him close and he kissed her. As she kissed him her tongue searched for his tonsils and he could taste the beer and the chicken. She smelt dirty but he wanted her too badly to stop now. She guided him into her. Within a few strokes Jamie had come and it was all over for him and all he wanted was to withdraw and escape from the sordid doorway.

"Is that it?" She sounded sarcastic which wasn't what she had intended. Jamie was the first person in ages that had bothered to talk to her and she had wanted sex with him. He had been kind and it was the first kindness she had experienced in a long time. "I didn't mean it like that," she said smiling at him, "is that the first time standing up?"

He felt foolish but simply said. "It's the first time, full stop."

"Well, next time will be better for both of us then."

With that she kissed him and walked in the unlocked door and was gone. He stood feeling stupid, pulling up his pants and trousers and then trudged home in the rain. As first sex it had been awful. It would have to be better than that, if not continuing masturbation would be the only route left; at least that was not so humiliating. He reached home and sat in a chair mulling over the night's events. He was still drunk but had sobered up enough to start wondering if tonight's sex might have been a bad idea.

He had not worn protection; he never carried it, as the prospect of sex was non-existent. He had worried all night about the fear of catching something and it worried him so much that he had gone on the web to read up on sexually transmitted diseases. For the next few months he examined his penis daily but no signs of disease appeared and he put this down as a stroke of good fortune. Whether or not he would ever get laid again he always carried a packet of three in his pocket in case.

He looked but never found the woman again either in the pub or when he went by that house. He didn't even know her name. The building had become boarded up and repossessed by the Council. Quite why this drunken woman, stayed on his radar he was not sure. Quite possibly because she was the only woman he'd ever been with.

***

It was a year before he saw her by chance sitting on the same bench in the park where they had eaten their takeaway. She looked terrible and may have been sleeping rough although she didn't have any belongings with her.

"Hi there, remember me? We never got on first name terms last time. I'm Jamie," he had said. She ventured no name so he didn't press the point.

She had looked up and studied his face for some time before she recognised him. She smiled, probably the first smile in a long time. He sat down beside her and they talked for some time.

"I was thrown out of the squat by the repossession and lost contact with the rest of the men. I got so desperate I even contemplated going home to see my mother, but courage failed me." She paused thoughtfully. "My mother's a social climber, would not have been able to cope with the state of her only daughter being such a failure."

Then she just clammed up as though it were all too much to bear. Jamie had offered to get some food and she readily accepted and they joked about sex afterwards without it being serious from either of them. For the next three weeks he met her and gave her some money for food and it was clear from the improvement in her appearance she was using the money for the right things. She was cleaner and had a few different clothes. She explained she was lodging with a bloke in return for sex but he had a girlfriend so there was nothing serious.

After a few more weeks she invited him to her digs and Jamie met the man. He took an instant dislike to him but he couldn't decide why. He had become attracted to her but was still reluctant to let her into his life on his own patch. He had no idea where that might lead. As he walked her early one evening to her house she invited him inside. The man was not in and Ruth showed him around. It was a truly depressing place and Jamie could not imagine living there. It contrasted sharply with his own comfortable surroundings. Her body language suggested this evening was heading towards sex and he went along with her suggestive conversation.

"You've been really nice to me. I thank you for that. Your thoughtfulness; you can't imagine what it means to someone in my position. I know it wasn't much the last time but I want to have sex with you here, now. Let me show what it can be like."

"I have had other sex since then you know." He lied and felt bad when he saw the hurt in her face. "I want sex with you but not because you feel sorry it wasn't great before."

"Look, if you don't want it, no skin off my nose. I like you and I'm grateful. It's the only way I can show it."

Jamie had moved toward her and they held each other, two sad cases in life reaching out for a chink of happiness together, however fleetingly. They moved upstairs to her room. Jamie was depressed at what he saw; an old eiderdown and a single pillow on a sagging single bed with no headboard. A single light bulb hung from a cracked ceiling with the remnants of a paper lantern shade. A chest of drawers was against one wall with peeling wallpaper and a table lamp, which she switched on after drawing the excuse for a curtain, which did not cover the whole window. The soft glow from the lamp made the room feel cosier, but only just. The wooden floor was bare save for a small rug by her bed and a chair in the corner. Ruth led him to the bed and they sat together side by side; she put her arm round his shoulders turning him towards her and kissed him gently on the mouth. It was so sensual Jamie felt arousal but did not want to rush things. There would be more time than in the alleyway.

He undid the buttons of her shirt, a man's shirt. Then he peeled back the shirt and she wriggled out of it. She reached behind and unclipped her bra. She let it drop to the floor. He found that act alone very sensual. He reached for her and pulled her close fondling her breasts. They were small but firm. He thought how much sexier they were than page three breasts. Her nipples were hard and he caressed them and pushed her back onto the bed and lay beside her. She undid the belt of her jeans and slid them down and hooked her fingers and pulled down her pants. Despite the last few weeks her body was very thin from lack of good food, her hipbones nearly piercing her skin. He could see her ribcage but she still excited him. He had never seen a naked body before and for the next few moments she would be his. He looked at her. Her face was much prettier than when he had first met her in the park. She was getting and looking better. He hoped he would be able to help her with more food. The bruises on her arms worried him. She noticed his concern and simply said. "Don't ask, don't spoil the moment."

Then she pulled away from him and knelt beside him on the bed. She undressed him and he enjoyed the way she led him into sex with her. He had produced a condom from his trouser pocket and she smiled and put it on him. She started to work him but he was scared he would come too quickly. He lay on top of her but not in her and they kissed passionately. For both it seemed the tensions of their lives, possibly similar, but endured separately, were set-aside for the moment. She encouraged him to enter her but he just lay fingering her and enjoyed her groans of pleasure. This was a new experience for him. Only his second time and yet he felt in control. For her, there had been many but maybe this was special. He entered her and she gasped at the size of him and as he ground into her he knew she was enjoying him. Jamie could not stop and he came. It had taken less than a minute. He lay panting on her and said "I'm sorry I couldn't hold it any longer."

"Don't say sorry. I'm enjoying you. Stay with me I'm coming myself."

Jamie lay there on her, his breathing in short pants and thoughts of how wonderful it had been. Ruth had him in a firm grip. She was bringing his erection back more strongly and they made love a second time. It was the most beautiful experience of his whole sad life and he lay there exhausted but happy. Then the mood changed suddenly as Ruth appeared nervous. Perhaps the man might return. Presumably she was his woman and Jamie got concerned. He wanted no trouble but neither did he want the moment to end.

"I'm sorry, Jamie. You'd better go in case he comes back."

Jamie did not argue. Perhaps he was scared too. He got dressed, turned to face her and said. "You were beautiful."

"You too, but go now."

"Will we meet up as usual in the park?"

"I'll be there."

"I don't even know your name."

"What's in a name?" With that she blew a kiss and ushered Jamie out of the room. He went downstairs and into the fresh early evening air. He felt like a new man. He had gone to the park everyday at various times over the next few months but she never showed up. He assumed he might never see her again.

***

The intercom clicked, it brought Jamie sharply back to the present. It was a deliveryman. He had a parcel for him in the lobby, which needed a signature. He opened the door and went downstairs still thinking about the women, could it be Ruth; was she this successful novelist? He was certain she was, it all tied in and if so he wondered whether their short acquaintance was in any way included in her books. He decided he would look at the web, just to find out more about her. Later that evening Jamie picked up the supplement again and read it more carefully. Ruth had been the only daughter of a wealthy family. Her father had gone to Eton and married a social climber, but the relationship had been turbulent with frequent rows and violence in which Ruth was frequently the target. Her father had committed suicide when his business had failed and Ruth had run away at sixteen to get away from her mother. She had lived on the streets and some years later she had been rescued after a failed suicide attempt and had been nursed back to health to lead a normal life. She had trained as a psychologist and had decided to write about the experiences in the form of a novel. She was currently a lay member of a Met Police study into violence within the family. Jamie was convinced from the photograph; this was his Ruth. It was all history now, but he was interested; he felt somehow his kindness to her may have helped. He felt good at the thought.

***

Jamie now started to go into the West End every morning and was becoming less nervous at the prospect. Life had changed. He wasn't certain why. Was it because he was out in the fresh air and not a virtual prisoner or was it that he was somehow in charge? In charge of his life and setting the pace, whatever the reason he like it and he found himself smiling in the mirror as he went out each day. He found it exhilarating to go with confidence and for these trips he had left the Maglite torch at home. This was real progress. He made sure not to use the same café where he had asked the waiter. He didn't want to draw attention to himself, although he wasn't certain why.

He called into the sandwich shop to buy lunch on two occasions and luckily on one day the man who he assumed was his father came in and joined the queue whilst Jamie was being served. The man must have been a valued customer; his sandwiches were ready and the girl serving Jamie called him forward and handed him his package.

"Here you are Frank, the bread is granary today, we've run out of white. Hope you don't mind."

Frank grunted, "I have no choice do I?" and walked out of the shop. No money was paid over. Jamie surmised he must have an account.

"Miserable sod," the girl said under her breath and smiled at Jamie, "thinks he owns the joint because he comes here every day and has an account."

"There's no pleasing some people." Jamie could not resist the observation and enjoyed being part of her conversation. He paid up and left the shop more certain than he had a right to be this was his father. He left the queue and went to a little area in a small square by some flats. There was a seat free and he sat and ate his sandwich thinking what to do next. He decided to wait until Frank closed the shop and to follow him to see where he lived. He had no idea where this might take him. If he caught a taxi that would be useless but if he got on a bus or the Underground then he would see what transpired.

April weather can be really bright and warm, but this was not one of these days. It had become dull and rain was in the air. He went for a walk and passed Frank's menswear shop and saw that the closing time was half past five. He went to the Underground and caught a train to go for a walk along the embankment. It was such a joy to see people enjoying themselves walking alongside the Thames but he had serious business. He returned to the shop about fifteen minutes before scheduled closing. It was lucky he had; Frank must have had a very quiet day and was closing early.

Frank walked to Warren Street Underground and Jamie followed at a discreet distance. He followed down the escalator and through the ticket barrier; his travel card would be good value today. They both got on a southbound Northern Line train that arrived within a couple of minutes. Frank sat in the middle of the carriage and Jamie stood at the end of the adjoining carriage so he had a clear view of him. As the train filled up at each station Jamie was worried he might lose sight of Frank but as people shoved past he held his ground so he could just see him.

Jamie had no idea where he would get off but at least he was on the same line as he normally used to get home. Then he almost missed Frank getting off and had to barge passed a couple kissing passionately in the doorway. It was Clapham South station and he almost fell from the train to the platform as he tripped on a bag. He looked back; the man still had his tongue down his girlfriend's throat. Luckily lots of passengers were also getting off as Jamie followed Frank to the exit signs. Once at street level he followed, not too far behind; again there were plenty of people about so he thought it most unlikely Frank would realise he was being followed.

They walked about fifteen minutes and then Frank turned up the path of a Victorian terraced house and opened the door and was gone. Jamie's heart was pounding. What a stroke of luck today had been. Not only was he almost certain he had identified his father, although he could not rationalise why he was so sure, but he'd also followed him to his home. He noted the address and decided that was enough for one day and retraced his steps before total darkness enveloped him and before, without his Maglite torch to comfort him, he lost confidence.

He arrived home at about eight o'clock and went inside to the sanctuary of his flat. He made himself coffee and sat in his favourite chair and watched as night closed in around him. What a day he had just had. What did he know for certain? Firstly he felt certain Frank was his father but would confronting him confirm it? Probably not. More than likely he would deny knowing his mother but showing him photos should bring some recognition, surely it would be impossible not show some reaction that Jamie would see as guilt. He knew from letters that Frank was a tailor and he was certain he had identified the right man in the photo whether or not he was his father. He also knew Frank's surname, Frank Michaels. It was on the top of the door of the shop proudly proclaiming his proprietorship of more than forty years.

He sat there mulling over his thoughts; he was exhausted. That night he slept the sleep of the dead.

Next day he hopped on the Underground the two stations from his home to Balham. He wanted to assess whether Frank lived alone and make a decision how, where and when he would confront him. It was raining hard and it was miserable. Jamie's jacket was not waterproof and the wetness was seeping onto his shoulders. He stuck it out for about half an hour before deciding he would attract attention to himself if he stayed around any longer. There appeared to be nobody else at the property but he had resisted the urge to walk up the path and ring the bell to find out. He repeated this every day for the remainder of the week and decided he would confront Frank at his own front door. Before he did so he needed to think out carefully what he would say and what he wanted to achieve by his actions.

He sat by his computer and pondered. Why was he doing this? He thought he had it clear in his mind. He wanted revenge against someone but what form could his revenge take. His father hadn't been necessary when his mother was alive but after her death he could, maybe should have been important.

So why revenge? It could all go wrong. He was not confident out there in the big wide world. The thought made him edgy. Perhaps he had stirred himself to taking action that could make his life worse. He thought for a long time. His coffee was cold. He got up and went to the kitchen and looked out at the street dark and foreboding and then he was certain he had to confront his father. The night of the beating came back regularly to haunt him and it was a monkey he had to get off his back. What if he actually found he liked his father? That worried him but he thought it unlikely and put it out of his thoughts. It still left the question; what was he going to say and achieve from the encounter. He poured himself a coffee and went to watch TV. This was a night to see what crime programmes were on the Discovery Channels. First he turned on the London news and caught the back end of an interview with a Detective called Strachan who was predicting a swift closure to the Tooting murder. Jamie thought the Police Inspector looked a little smug and the end of the interview it was explained a chance lead from a member of the public would bring the case to a swift close.

Jamie wondered where in Tooting this crime had taken place; he had seen no increased police activity in the area and he had walked to Tooting station every day that week.

Chapter 11

Three months had passed since his beating and Jamie was getting impatient with himself. He kept going over and over in his mind what he thought he wanted to do. Maybe he was trying to plan in too great a detail. At the minimum he wanted nothing more than to find out whether Frank Michaels was his father. Did it matter whether his idea for revenge, so deviously plotted on his computer became second fiddle or even a non-starter? He needed to know.

"Bugger it," he shouted at his computer, "let's get on with this or I'll end up back where I started."

He felt better. He had made a decision. He would confront Frank on his doorstep late in the evening when it was dark and let events take their course. He felt strangely elated at his bold decision. No more prevarication, no more planning, he would go to his father and talk to him.

He set out the next afternoon to be in the street near the shop and follow him home as he had done before. He took with him a photograph from his mother's album; the one with Frank's name written on the back and taken at the seaside with his mother. He also took a copy of the part of the letter in which his mother had described to her sister about Frank and his menswear shop. This would be pretty conclusive proof of the relationship but not necessarily that Frank was his father.

Jamie hung around the street and promptly at half past five Frank appeared on the street locking up for the night. There was a real routine about Frank and it pleased Jamie there appeared to be no other staff working in the shop. Like him, Frank was a loner. He followed the same route and reached the house but it was still light so Jamie hung around for nearly two hours. It didn't get dark normally until nearly half past eight but this was a dismal evening. Nobody was about so he walked down the road and turned up the path. Mercifully the overgrown bushes masked his presence on the doorstep. He was invisible to the neighbours.

His heart was pounding and he was sweating. "What am I doing here?" he said under his breath. He waited. It seemed ages before he plucked up courage. He rang the bell but couldn't hear any sound. He waited. Perhaps it wasn't working. He suddenly felt out of his depth. Panic gripped him and he turned. He could just walk away. This was not a good idea. How had he convinced himself it might be? He unzipped his jacket to cool down. The Maglite torch in the pocket made his jacket swing open. His mouth was dry and he felt faint and nauseous. "Oh God," he muttered under his breath, "This is all going wrong."

He heard a noise and a light came on. Through the frosted glass he sensed someone was coming down the stairs. Jamie came to his senses and he knew he must be strong and keep the initiative. The door opened and there before him was Frank Michaels. He looked older and more dishevelled than he had imagined from his sightings in the sandwich shop and following him home. He wore an old cardigan and was still wearing a business shirt with tie but had changed into a dirty old pair of trousers. How incongruous he looked for a tailor. Worse, what a pathetic figure, if he was his father.

Jamie felt disgust and without thinking pushed Frank back into the hall and quickly stepped inside and slammed the front door.

"What the hell do you think you're doing? Who are you?"

"Shut up and move down the hall."

Frank resisted and Jamie lashed out with the Maglite torch. It hit Frank a glancing blow on the side of the head and he fell against the wall and slid slowly to the floor. Jamie panicked. He hadn't intended to hurt him in this way although the likelihood of violence had been a possibility. Frank lay there motionless but was breathing. He had a nasty welt on the side of his face. He wasn't a big man but neither was Jamie, so getting him to sit against the wall was not easy.

It was then Jamie realised he had been suckered; Frank was not unconscious and he lashed out and caught him straight in the gut. Jamie doubled over and fell on Frank and they struggled on the floor. He was amazed how strong he was. He took him for a decrepit old man but he fought hard. He hit Jamie again, it caught him in the ribs and it hurt. They struggled and gradually Jamie got the upper hand. He forced Frank away and made a grab for his torch that had dropped to the floor, but the old man was surprisingly quick and kicked it away. Jamie was now angry. This was not going to plan. This was meant to be a push over. He wondered if he had badly misjudged his father. He even had a sneaking admiration but it was too late for that. He was there only to confront and humiliate him. To get revenge was the plan, not to fight for his life. Finally, Jamie got free and hit him in the face. Blood poured from his nose and suddenly he felt him weakening. Frank still came at him and lunged with his arm straight and hand held open. His plan was to gouge Jamie's eyes but he was now too slow. Jamie grabbed at his hand. He caught hold of his thumb and bent it violently backwards.

He heard a snap and Frank screamed in pain. All the fight was now gone and he was too weak. He slumped to the floor. Jamie picked up the torch and hit him again. He was not going to be suckered a second time. This time he was out for the count. Jamie stood there, his chest heaving, fighting for breath. The fight had been unavoidable but it changed everything. He was now on a path from which there would be no return. He could just leave whilst his father was unconscious. The likelihood of him identifying Jamie was small. It wasn't what Jamie needed. He needed to talk to his father and humiliate him; revenge, pain was what Jamie needed to regain control of his life.

He dragged Frank into the kitchen and sat him on the floor. He found a roll of tailor's tape and scissors on the kitchen table and bound his hands in front of him and then his feet. He went to the sink and picked up a tea towel. He was thinking he would tie it around Frank's mouth. He didn't want any shouting to arouse the neighbours. For the moment he just held it in his hand.

Jamie sat on a chair; he was still breathing hard, sweating and his heart was racing, but he felt strangely in control. It had not occurred to him what would happen if a neighbour by chance called round to see Frank, but there was no point in worrying now. Frank appeared to be stirring. He opened his eyes. They were full of fear. Jamie now understood what it was like to hold power over another person. He liked the sensation; it was new to him.

Jamie was forming in his mind what he wanted to say. Frank lapsed into unconsciousness again. He wondered what he would do once he had questioned Frank. What was the end of this evening going to bring; he couldn't now just walk away leaving him bound and gagged. Someone would find Frank and Jamie had made no attempt to conceal his face although Frank at this point might have no clue who he was. This was getting complicated.

Jamie's panic grew. He hadn't thought through how this might pan out. All he had focussed on was revenge and somehow to humiliate his father; it hadn't occurred to him he might have get violent to do so.

Frank groaned and slowly opened his eyes. The welts on the side of his head were already looking angry. Jamie stared at him.

"Do you have any idea who I am?"

Frank moved his head from side to side.

"My name is Jamie and my mother and you were friends." Jamie felt pathetic as he wondered how to say what he wanted. He picked out a photograph of Frank and his mother and showed it to him. Jamie could not be sure but there appeared to be no flicker of emotion or recognition on Frank's face. "Do you recognise yourself?"

He nodded.

"Do you recognise this woman?"

No reaction.

"I'll ask you again, do you know this woman?"

"Yes."

"Who is she?"

"I knew her a long time ago. I can't remember her name."

"Her name was Carol."

"So? What's it to do with me?"

"Do you know you are my father?" Jamie blurted out the words.

"I don't know you. I don't know why you've broken into my house."

"Shut up and listen."

"Why? Why should I do what you say?"

"Do you want me to hit you again?"

The old man looked defeated. What might have started as defiance was now reduced to cowering. "Tell me what you want."

"I have to know whether you are the person who my mother knew. Are you the man in the photo?"

"Yes, I knew your mother, but that was years ago."

"Thirty five years ago to be precise and that's how old I am."

"So what, your mother knew loads of men. Do you know what she did for a living?"

Jamie's anger flared. His mother was not a prostitute before he was born. He had held the cherished belief she only became a prostitute to make enough money to bring him up.

"Shut up. I know what my mother became. She told me when she died. She told me my father abandoned her when she became pregnant."

"Hold on a minute. I never lived with your mother. We went out together quite often. I used to take her down to Margate in the summer. That's where that picture was taken, but we never lived together."

"Shut up. Don't keep denying it. You are my father. I don't want anything from you, anything to do with you but I have to know."

"How did you find me anyway?"

"In my mother's effects was a letter to her sister. It said you ran a tailoring shop in Marylebone Lane. She said your name was Frank and that it was a tragedy you had never taken responsibility for me."

Frank's expression changed from defiant denial to one of total resignation. Further prevarication would be useless, but he wasn't finished yet. "Well you won't know from me. I never knew she was really pregnant. She often used to joke about it; probably to make me marry her."

"What do you mean?"

"Women like that often tried to break out by trapping a bloke."

Frank never saw it coming; the torch hit him again and he slumped to the floor unconscious.

"Bastard. You bastard." Jamie shouted to the lifeless form in front of him. His head was swimming. This had all gone wrong. What he really wanted was to hear was Frank was his father and he was sorry he abandoned him. Jamie sat back wondering what to do next. The old man stirred; saliva was trickling from his mouth and a stain appeared on the fly of his trousers.

Jamie took a much closer look at Frank. His colour had changed and his breathing had become laboured. He had no idea what was happening; maybe this was a trick to get him to untie him and then Frank would fight back. Frank started to jerk. Jamie thought he might be having a heart attack.

Jamie untied his hands and feet and helped Frank to lay straight on the floor. He had no idea of how much time had elapsed but it was clear Frank was in serious trouble and needed a doctor. He rushed to the phone on the wall to dial for an ambulance. He picked up the receiver and the dialling tone made him freeze. How was he going to explain this? He replaced the receiver and looked down at Frank who was now lying motionless on the kitchen floor. The heaving of his chest had stopped. Was he dying or was he already dead? He felt for a pulse but couldn't find one. He had no idea whether he was feeling in exactly the right place. He was deathly still, no movement at all. He looked around the room and there was a small mirror on the wall. He lifted it off the hook and held it close to Frank's face. There was no breath but still he could not be certain.

He sat on a chair in a funk. What the hell was he to do next? He felt guilty. He was not sure, had he intended harm or just humiliation. Did he feel guilty? Had he been responsible for Frank's death? Had he murdered him? How could he know he had a weak heart? Mostly he felt cheated, cheated of knowing definitely, one way or another, whether Frank was his father.

He bent down and touched the body, there was no movement, no breathing and no pulse; either in his wrist or in his neck. Frank was dead.

How could he conceal what had happened? He looked at the body and whilst there were no marks to suggest he had been bound and gagged there was the problem of the bruises on the side of his head. He toyed with the idea of placing Frank near an overturned chair next to the tall cupboard so that it might look as though he had fallen and banged his head. This was unlikely to be convincing. There were three separate wounds and what about the broken thumb. All this time anger was welling inside him.

"Why did he have to die? All I wanted was to know if it was him and to make him feel bad." Then Jamie snapped. Frustration welled up into anger. He lashed out at the lifeless body lying prostrate on the floor. He pounded the body with his fists and seeing the heavy tailor's scissors he had used to cut Frank's bonds he grabbed them and stabbed Frank in the chest, not once but repeatedly until he was exhausted. He was crying; he didn't know whether it was remorse or anger. He slumped back and lent against a cupboard door.

There was no blood spurting everywhere. This was a lifeless corpse; blood only seeped from the wounds and covered the blades of the scissors and his hands. Suddenly Jamie gained control of his emotions. Now he would be classed as a murderer. He needed to cover his tracks and get out of there. He had not come to kill Frank, but he was dead anyway and Jamie was responsible. He washed his hands in the sink and dried them on the tea towel. He gathered up the tapes he had cut loose. He found a carrier bag in the cupboard and put all the evidence in the bag, carefully wrapping the scissors, which he had washed in a clean tea towel. He would dispose of these later. He went through his movements and wiped the door handles and phone. He checked the room and switched off the lights. He reached the front door and checked outside. There was nobody around and he walked through the door, turned and wiped the bell push and strode down the path and into the street.

Now he was amazingly calm. No pounding heart, no sweaty palms. He walked normally not drawing attention to himself. He decided to walk; not to catch the Underground the two stops back to Tooting Broadway. He did not want to be part of any CCTV footage that might be checked over later once the body was found.

He walked calmly. He was not experiencing the fear he would normally feel being out on the street at night. Was this act the one that released him from the hell he had endured for over twenty years? Nevertheless the 'Maglite' torch in his hand comforted him. The carrier bag knocked against his leg, the gruesome contents he would need to deal with as soon as possible. He wondered how he would clean the scissors and the torch before dumping them and where would he do that? The fresh air was remarkable. He felt invigorated and wondered how long the feeling might last before he descended into panic at what he had done. It started to rain and he zipped up his jacket but decided not to put up his hood. He hated the 'hoodie' culture but more importantly he feared it made being stopped randomly by a policeman more likely.

At last, he turned the corner into his road. He would be home in five minutes. He would be safe, at least for now. Then he saw a policeman coming towards him and his heart missed a beat. His inclination was to cross the road but the policeman might think he had something to hide. He was getting closer. Jamie's mouth was dry and he was starting to panic. He had no idea what to do if the policeman stopped him. What would he say if asked what he was doing and where was he going. He was now just yards away.

"Evening sir, it's going to be a nasty night."

"Yes." Jamie blurted and just kept walking. Then he was clear. He dared not look round. He could not hear footsteps behind him so he sneaked a look behind as though he planned to cross the road. The policeman was just turning the corner. He was sweating profusely and started to feel nauseous. He had to get home and quickly. At last he was at the entrance to his flats and he entered the door code and walked into the lobby. He almost ran up the stairs and inserted the key into his front door and slid inside the darkened room, lit only by the streetlight opposite. He walked into the bathroom but before he could get to the basin he was violently sick.

Chapter 12

Jamie sat slumped over the toilet basin. He was still being sick. He was kneeling in his vomit on the floor and the place stank. The feeling passed after about five minutes and he got up and started to mop up the mess. He needed a shower and stood under the hot stinging water for a long time. His clothes were in a heap as he towelled himself off. He decided that all the clothes he had worn had to go but he wasn't sure how to dispose of them. Firstly he put them in the washing machine with the tea towels. Even his favourite jacket would have to go. He padded around in his bathrobe and started to feel better. The nausea had passed.

He washed the scissors and the barrel of the torch. He even washed the carrier bag but had no idea whether this would get rid of all the blood or other evidence that might be traced to him or Frank. He decided that the clothes and scissors and torch all had to be separately disposed of and he would do that the next night; but where he had no idea.

He suddenly felt hungry. It was now ten and he hadn't eaten since a snack for lunch. He sat down with beans on toast and turned on the 'Ten o' clock News'. He would need to examine the papers and listen for any reports of Frank's death. There would be no reason for anything tonight unless somebody had called at the house or a neighbour reported hearing noises or an unusual occurrence. There was no point in dwelling on it; waves of tiredness swept over him and he fell asleep in the chair.

Next morning Jamie planned the disposal. He decided to catch the Underground and head over the River into North London. He would walk along a canal path and throw the scissors and torch into the water. He reasoned that as canals were not tidal there was a chance they would sink in the mud and remain undetected. The clothes he would burn somewhere, again he had no idea where. He had toyed with the idea of giving the clothes to beggars sleeping rough but the risk of being identified later was too great.

This was the plan and he set out to carry it out with everything in separate carrier bags. If stopped, it would look as though he were going to the launderette. He got on the Northern line and headed for Camden Town station. He walked up Camden High Street; following signs to the canal and then along the towpath for a long way but there were always people around. If he threw the scissors or torch somebody might remember and this was dangerous. He might need to come back under the cover of darkness. Finally he reached a stretch where a couple were sitting on a bench, more interested in each other, than anything around them. They were kissing and he could see no other people on the canal path although for all he knew thousands of eyes could be watching him from canal side properties. There would never be a perfect moment. He did not relish having to come back especially at night and he threw the scissors into the middle of the canal. He also picked up some stones and threw them, not the usual activity for a man but what the hell. He felt better. He had got rid of the scissors and later he did the same with the torch, but some miles further on near the City Road Basin.

His decision on disposing his bag of clothes was made easy. A refuse lorry was collecting in the street as he came off the towpath and he lobbed it in the back whilst nobody was looking. Whether this was as safe as burning he had no idea but probably it would be lost in some landfill site forever. Good or bad decision? What the hell, it was now done and he could walk free from the fear of being stopped.

Jamie arrived home relieved but pleased with his day. He sat with a coffee in front of his computer and looked at the word 'Revenge' logo dripping in blood. He had actually done it. He'd fought back. Frank died because he had a heart attack, but Jamie had brought it on. He was increasingly getting a buzz from what he'd done. He'd actually taken it to the next level. He had stabbed the corpse. He assumed that to the police that would make him the same as any other killer.

He looked at himself in a mirror. "Was Frank my father?" He asked himself. "Yes. I'm almost positive. The letter and the photo; they are conclusive enough." He laughed at the absurdity of talking to a mirror; but he craved the chance to talk about what he had done. He had nobody. There was no accomplice to share this with; somebody implicated who would need to keep the secret with him. He was alone and would now have to wait to see what news coverage there was so he could get some thrill out of reading about it but he was to be disappointed. There was nothing on TV, nothing in the national papers or the locals. Was it a conspiracy or perhaps the body had not been discovered yet? He waited for days. It was agony.

Then he saw it on BBC London news. A reporter was standing outside a house in a suburban street. He turned up the volume:

".... the body was found in this house today in Balham. Police confirm he had been dead for two or perhaps three days. The man, who lived alone, was Frank Michaels, aged 60. He ran a small menswear shop in London and was reported missing by the sandwich store next to his premises when he hadn't opened up as usual. Police are saying nothing about how he died but that foul play was suspected.

"I have with me Detective Sergeant Williamson of the local Police. Detective Sergeant, can you tell us yet how Mr Michaels died and what motive there might be?"

"No, I'm sorry I can't. Until we have the Pathologist's report and have carried out further examination of the house I'm not able to add anything."

"Can you tell us whether the occupant has been murdered?"

"There are aspects regarding this death that to talk about might prejudice our enquiries and so at this stage I am not in a position to say how the occupant died."

"Do you have any leads at all?"

"Not at this stage. I'm sorry I cannot say anymore at this point in time. Until we have the pathologist's report it is useless to speculate. I would ask that if any member of the public saw anything unusual happening in this street over the last few days then they should contact their local police who will route the calls to us."

"Thank you, Detective Sergeant Williamson and with that I hand you back to the studio."

Jamie had watched fascinated and now he wanted to know whether that would be all or would there be further news later; was it important enough to warrant more coverage. He decided he would make it so.

He spread all the newspapers on the floor and cut out letters to construct a letter he would send to a national daily paper. He sat at the computer and drafted a message. It took him over an hour to think it through then wearing a pair of rubber gloves as he cut out the letters and pasted the letter together. It read:

'Ask the police why the dead man in Balham had a broken thumb.'

He put the message carefully in an envelope, which he lifted, from the middle of a batch he had in a drawer. Wearing his gloves he addressed it to the 'Crime Editor, Daily Mail' at their offices in London. He decided not to post it locally but do so the next morning when he was planning to go into London.

Chapter 13

Strachan was sitting quietly at his desk. It had been an unusually quiet start to the day. He was reading the incident report of the killing in Balham the previous week. Although the second murder in the same area within weeks it was not a case for his office and was being dealt with locally. He wondered what the pathologist report had said. There had been no further news coverage, which was good in one sense. It left the local boys to investigate without pressure. The phone rang.

"Boss. I've got a Crime reporter from the Daily Mail. Jim, something, says he knows you."

"Put him through."

"Hello, George. Got something of interest to you lot. Thought I'd give you first shout."

"OK, what is it?"

"First, are you involved with this Balham killing?"

"Not yet but sounds like I might be now."

"What can you tell me about the case?"

"Nothing. You know how this works. We've been over the course a few times. You tell me what you have and I'll decide if it's relevant and if it is, you get first shout before the rest. That's it so tell me or stop wasting my time."

George always knew Jim would have to tell him. He'd had some tasty morsels from him before. He had built up a reputation as one of the smartest and best crime reporters on the street. Not for him the cushy job of Crime Editor which could have been his for the asking on most other papers. His was a street investigation job and he loved it.

"OK. I'm wearing surgical gloves. I opened a letter addressed to my boss. He's away. I'll read it:

'Ask the police why the dead man in Balham had a broken thumb.'

That's all it says; so what's it about."

"I've no idea it's not my case but by the time you get here with it I'll know more."

"You mean come over now. It's not convenient."

"Make it convenient. There'll be a pass waiting for you downstairs."

"There better be something in it for me. Half an hour. Cheerio."

Strachan was immediately on the phone to the Chief Super. "Boss, I've some information on the Balham case. Who's handling it?"

"What sort of information?"

Strachan related the phone call.

"It's your case now. Tell Local it's being moved here but not why. If you get flak refer them to me. Get up to speed and bring Jim up when he's here. Bring forensics with you."

Strachan called the local Police; surprisingly there was no argument and the papers would be faxed immediately. DS Williamson would be available later for a personal debrief but he was not available at present.

Strachan felt somewhat sorry to have to take their case away. Scotland Yard were the bogeymen to local coppers but he didn't sound unhappy so perhaps they were too busy with other cases.

The papers dribbled through from the fax over the next five minutes. There wasn't much except the pathologist report that confirmed four key facts which had not come out in the coverage. First that Frank Michaels was dead before he was stabbed, second, he had head wounds third, his thumb was broken and last there had been a struggle. The likely weapon was a pair of heavyweight scissors used by tailors.

Interviews with the sandwich shop had not really added anything to the fact he was a tailor with this one shop, although he had owned a chain some years earlier and he was a creature of habit in his sandwich choice. No other details could be gleaned that was of any apparent use in finding out why he had died or who had plunged the scissors repeatedly into the body.

Strachan thought this might be an interesting case. Jim arrived carrying the envelope and message in a sealed plastic bag that he had probably pinched from a police department on one of his many visits.

"Hi Jim. Come in and sit down. Coffee?"

"White, with please."

"This is Sandy, she's forensic and will be taking this away. Have you photo copied it?"

"Come on George. I'm no amateur. That might damage forensics' job but I trust you not to cut me out of this story.

"I find that difficult to believe your paper would let it out of their hands without a copy."

"OK fair cop; I did take a photograph of it with my phone camera, but held it with tweezers. So what's the score?"

"The score is we are off to see the boss."

"Sounds important."

"We have no idea but someone wants us to know about an aspect of crime there is always more to it than meets the eye."

They went along the corridor and knocked on the door; the sign read Chief Superintendent Victor Galliard.

"He'll be French then?" Jim quipped as a voice shouted to enter.

The boss's office, although large, was filled with filing cabinets and a bookcase and his desk was stacked with reports.

"You'll be Jim; we've not met have we? Nothing personal but I keep away from the press if I can. Thanks for coming and whatever George has promised you I shan't interfere but for the moment a 'DA' Notice will be slapped on this case so nothing is going into the public domain until George has been down to the crime scene and been debriefed by the locals. Understood?"

"Understood," Jim acknowledged but he wanted to remind the Chief Super that 'DA' notices had no legal significance anymore and Editors could ignore them, but there was no point in arguing; George had promised him a head start on the story.

***

Strachan walked under the blue police tape and up the path. A detective was standing at the door.

"Good Morning, D. S. Williamson. Are you D. I. Strachan?"

George produced his warrant card and they walked inside. It was an old Victorian house, typical of thousands in the area. He got through to the kitchen and saw the marks where the body had been found.

"Was it you who came when the house was opened up?"

"Uniformed came. They confirmed there had been no forced entry. A locksmith was called to open up and I came and I was the first inside."

"Was the body face up or down?"

"Face up. He was not soaked in blood despite the stab wounds with a thick blade; likely heavy scissors according to the pathologist. Michaels was a tailor so he would have a pair around."

"But none were found?"

"No. As the report says he was dead when the stabbings occurred. Heart attack probably. The killer may have been known to him as he opened the door to him."

"The killer could have been already here." Strachan did not want to jump to early conclusions.

"Whatever. There was a struggle. Here in the hall and then he was dragged to the kitchen. Whether he was dead already or not we've no idea. The key thing to me is that all prints have been cleaned off so the killer was careful. May have been a pro."

"What, a contract kill?"

"Possibly but I've no clear fix at the moment. Anyway that's your problem now," he said, not meaning to be ungracious.

Strachan ignored the jibe. No need to rub Williamson's nose in it. He was reluctant at this stage to tell him about the note to the press. It became apparent he would have to when Williamson asked, "Why has this been moved up to you. Is there a development we don't know about?"

"Yes, but for you only until I say otherwise. Agreed?"

"Okay."

"A newsman I know rang to say he had received a cut out message asking about a broken thumb on the Balham victim. No mention was made by you in the TV coverage or any press reports so it has to be the killer."

"The killer wants some publicity given to this that identifies it as 'his' victim?"

"That's it. These escalate into messy cases. So no offence to you but we have the resources and that's why I'm here."

"Well, that's a relief. Thought for a moment we weren't trusted."

"Not so. I want you on the case for all local work. You're seconded. I've told your boss and why."

"Thanks, a bit of excitement will be good for a change."

"Sorry no more TV interviews. Pass everything to my office and direct to me. Here's my mobile number. Anything else I need to know?"

"No. There appears to be no attempt to search for anything. No mess upstairs but we have no idea if anything's missing. The initial 'path' report is the most we have and the photos should now be on your desk."

"Sir." The voice of D.S. Grayson cut through from the front door. "I've got a set of trainer footprints off the flower bed by the door. I'm taking a caste now. We've searched and the victim has no trainers so it might be something."

"Good. I need to get back," he turned to Williamson, "what's your first name?"

"Dick."

"I need you at the Yard. Can you bring Grayson back to town when she's finished? She'll get you ID for access to our floor."

"Of course."

"OK. I'll keep you posted but remember what you now know is not for chatting to your mates. We need this evidence kept quiet for the moment."

Strachan walked out to his car and was driven back to his office.

***

Strachan walked to his desk. There were yellow and pink 'post it' notes all on his pile of papers, which included the photographs. He picked the pink first. His number two, Gemma always got his attention first. Gemma had the knack of cutting through trivia and he always knew exactly what he needed from a few words on her trademark pink notes. She cut through all the minutiae. On this occasion he was totally wrong. The note said 'Sam rang re lunch next week'.

None of the other notes were particularly important so he grabbed a coffee from the machine and sat to take stock. The phone rang.

"Jim, Any developments?"

"Sorry Jim. You'll have to be patient. The deal stands."

"My boss has rung in. I've opened his mail. I always do and he knows it but this is the hottest thing ever."

"Tell him to ring me. I'll square it, but you've got to trust me. Nothing to be published. That was the deal."

"OK but he won't be pushed around."

"I'll speak to him, where is he?"

"At home."

Strachan wrote down the number. He would ring in a while but he needed to get his thoughts about this set down on his pad. His yellow legal pad was his trademark in the department. Everyone else used standard issue white. He wandered up to the Chief's office, knocked but entered an empty room. He'll brief him later.

Chapter 14

Strachan dialled the number he knew without having to check. "Hello Mrs Jacobs. How's my favourite plump lady?" He knew how Sam loved the name she had taken when she married Eddie.

"Hi to you George. What gives?"

"Is that slang or do you really want to know what I'm doing?"

"You sound a bit prickly today."

"Sorry but got a big new case on. Murder in Balham."

"I saw it on TV. Why you, isn't it for the local boys?"

"Initially just because it's the second killing in the area. It's unconnected but there's a development which ratchets it up for me to make my name on."

"Oh do tell."

"Sorry not at the moment, but I should be able to when we have lunch. I'm going to be busy but if you can accept being put off at short notice let's put it in the diary for Wednesday, usual time. I should be able to tell you by then."

"It'll have to do then. How are you and Madge?"

"Madge keeps asking when she is going to see you. She wants it to be before the baby arrives?"

"We now have the definite date for the lunch party here so I'll be able to chat with her then. Would you like me to ring her?"

"Yes please. That'll get me brownie points if you ring her. Brilliant. So I'll see you on Wednesday. Sandwiches OK?"

"I suppose so. Nobody seems to do lunch anymore."

"Must go now. Bye. Give our love to Eddie.

***

Eddie was just finishing a meeting when Sam rang.

"Hi darling. Everything OK with you. Just had George on the phone. He's got a big murder case on. It was on TV the other night. In Balham."

"So?"

"So nothing. Just chatting. The date for the lunch party is agreed. You do have it in your office diary?"

"Is that all you rang me for? The answer's the same as the last time you asked."

"Don't get so snooty. Can't I ring my children's father to see he is okay? They keep asking me."

"Very funny now get off the phone unless you have something important to say otherwise I shan't be home in time for dinner." He put the phone down before Sam had a chance to continue.

She stuck her tongue out as she replaced the receiver. "Men. No romance."

***

Sam followed her routine on the days she went to see George; dropping the kids with her mum and then dashing for the train into London. She still never allowed enough time.

She breezed into Scotland Yard and collected her pass. She was amazed how many people still seemed to know who she was. It was a comfortable feeling and she liked it.

George as ever was waiting at the lift and gave her an exaggerated hug to encompass her and the bulge.

"You sure this isn't another set of twins?" She kissed him despite people looking on. She loved it; the look of embarrassment in a hardened cop was a joy to behold. He knew it and played along.

"Come in and take the weight of your feet."

"Are you saying I'm overweight?"

"If the cap fits, wear it. Now sandwiches are here and coffee's coming." They chatted about life in the department and common friends. Sam asked how Juan was getting on.

"Juan is doing fine. He's well respected here and I hear a rumour, but you must promise me not to say anything, I think he might stay permanently."

"That's wonderful. I do love him so. It's feels like I've known him forever and he's so special. I really fear for him if he had to go back to Peru. I haven't told you but I even asked Eddie if he could find a role for him in the business. With his Spanish and Eddie's got quite a few projects in Spain it could have been ideal."

"Juan's a copper Sam. Always was and always will be. It's in his genes. Nice thought though. He'd be impressed and grateful."

"You mustn't tell him George. That'd be awful. He'd think I was trying to run his life."

"He wouldn't mind. If Eddie wasn't around he'd be after you himself."

Sam blushed and laughed. "Give him my love."

"That reminds me. Rumour has it he has a girlfriend in the force. She's a sergeant. They've been seen out two or three times in the past fortnight."

"Who is it?"

"I've no idea actually. It's his business."

"How infuriating men are. You ought to know."

"Why, ought I to know?"

"Because."

"Because why?"

"Just because I want to know, and so should you if she's one of your people."

"There's no answer to that!"

"Anyway it's wonderful. Perhaps he would like to bring her to the lunch party. I'll ask him if he would like to bring anyone, without letting on I know."

"I bet he'll easily see through that. Now there's someone working here I think you'd like to meet. She's a bit of a celebrity. Her name is Ruth and she has been seconded to this department. She's a psychologist specialising in violence to children in the home. Would you like to chat with her when we're done?"

"Be nice to talk to a female every now and then."

"I'll call her down." He rang and Ruth said she would be along in about ten minutes. "She is quite famous. There was a colour supplement on her. She suffered badly from abuse and lived rough. Then an incident changed her life and she got her life back and trained. She became very successful and decided to write a novel which was based on her own experience."

"Why not an autobiography?"

"Ask her. Anyway she has served on working groups on these issues and her book may be made into a film. She has been asked to raise the profile of the issues within the force."

"Now tell me about this case before she gets here."

"This is still hush-hush. Nobody outside a few people knows of this development." George explained about the phone call from the newspaper and the message. "It's looking like this one has some way to run. It's as though the killer wants his signature on this. It suggests as though there may be more to come."

"Any leads?"

"Nothing. No murder weapon, no finger prints, no reason why this man, a tailor, never married, lived alone and ran a menswear shop should be targeted."

"Sounds very professional but perhaps a grudge. So nothing to go on?"

"A footprint but it might be the postman, milkman or anyone. We're checking."

Ruth appeared at the door and George introduced her. "Ruth this is Sam, ex copper, family friend and very gutsy lady. Sam this is Ruth. I've told Sam about you and thought it would be nice for you to meet.

Sam had eaten her sandwich and was finishing her coffee. The phone rang. She could see a concerned look on George's face.

"Gotta go. Needed upstairs. The press are chasing to see if we are making progress. You two have a chat. Sam can see herself out?" George gathered a file of papers, leaned over and kissed Sam on the cheek and walked out.

"Hi. I feel I know you. George never stops talking about you and I've also read about you. George has a picture of your medal ceremony on the notice board."

"I got a medal and another officer lost his life on the same job." Sam did not want to talk about it.

"Sorry, didn't mean to pry.

"No please, it's just raw when I think the bastard who did it is still at large."

"I understand you brought Juan Ramos to England." Ruth said to lighten the moment.

"Not quite brought but I asked if he could come. His life was in danger and I owe him my life. Simple as that."

"Not so simple. I've been around here about six months and I'm fascinated by the way the police work. If the general public understood your dedication you wouldn't hear half the criticism that seems to be thrown as it is now. George told me about Peru."

Sam didn't want to talk about herself. She was consumed with interest about Ruth. "Tell me what made you become a psychologist. I've not seen the supplement you were featured in."

"I'll give you the short version." Ruth explained about her childhood and the abuse from her mother that amounted to violence and occasionally resulted in it.

"After my father committed suicide I had to leave. If I hadn't I would probably have followed him. I led a life living rough, in squats, with druggies and I was still getting beaten up. I was going downhill fast. Then one year, I was about twenty-five I met this guy in a pub. He was a loner. We talked a lot. He didn't know his father; he'd jumped ship when his mother got pregnant. He suffered from bullying. He was not what you would say, good looking; he was only just over five feet, so I suspect this compounded his problems. Anyway, he bought the drinks and after the pub closed he offered to buy a take away. It was my first real meal in weeks. We were both drunk and on the way home from the pub and to say thanks I had sex with him. It turned out it was his first time."

Sam was shocked but intrigued.

"I didn't see him again for ages and we met again by chance when I was at rock bottom. He said his name was Jamie. I was sleeping in a house and paid the owner with sex although he had a girlfriend. He used to beat me for no reason but that was my normal existence. Anyway Jamie used met me in the park and always gave me money for food and a few clothes. He was really nice, never asked for anything in return. I had been forming a plan; it had been evolving during this time with Jamie. I would try and get myself sorted out. I needed to get help. It was his kindness that gave me the strength and I grew really fond of him. I had decided the day I was going to leave and I knew I had to sever links with him. I felt guilty I would be leaving and I had sex with him again. This time it was really beautiful."

"What happened then?"

"It was his kindness which was a life saver. It brought me to my senses. His thoughtfulness in those few weeks had given me the resolve to do something to get out but I needed to make a clean break. Jamie would have been baggage."

"So what did you do?"

"I went to see the Nun's in my old school and see if they would help me. They were fabulous; they put me in touch with a charity and I was sorted out. It took over a year before I felt in control of my life. I'm not sure why I'm telling you all this."

"Some story and now you're famous. It's lovely. Ever wondered whatever happened to him?"

"Jamie? Yes often; but life moves on. I do owe him, he really did save my life and he has no idea. It would be nice if I could thank him but I wouldn't know where to start."

"Best left I would think. Look, I need to be going. Pick the kids up and get the man's meal. It's a tough life. I do hope we get to chat again, I'd love to hear the rest."

"Next time you come we'll have another chat. I'm here for a while longer and you seem to come in quite a lot."

"Can't live without it. Bye."

Ruth went out and Sam headed for home. What a story to tell Eddie.

Chapter 15

Strachan had the team in the squad room in front of a clipboard. Each detective was reporting on his particular line of enquiry. He opened up with the latest from the Pathologist.

"Appears there was one hell of a struggle. The assailant hit Michaels at least a couple of times with something round, and heavy enough to cause bad wounds. He was dead from a heart attack before he was stabbed. Indicates a crime of passion, the killer probably got angry he died before it was planned. It says the struggle was violent and we have hair and skin on the body so we can get DNA. We're waiting to hear if it matches anyone with previous."

Strachan waited for the murmur of comment that usually would follow when his team started to come up with its own thoughts. He could hear a pin drop.

"Geoff, what have you got from where he worked?" Geoff was a career D.C. Soon to retire; he simply loved routine investigation work. He liked to be told what to do, but once he was out there not much escaped him.

"Not much. There are two places where I got real helpful stuff, naturally the sandwich bar next to his shop. They're the ones who called in. They were worried he was missing. They say he never took holidays and if he was having a day off then he rang or told them before to cancel his sandwich order. The girl on the counter noticed a man loitering outside on a number of occasions. Thought it was odd but then one day he came in and bought something so she then put it out of her mind. Perhaps he had been uncertain before but now he was a customer."

"Did she give you a description?"

"Short and ugly."

"What do you mean, short and ugly?"

"Precisely that. She says he was pale, had a cap so she couldn't see his hair colour, bomber jacket and the counter obscured the rest."

"Why this man?"

"Well it was at the same time as Michaels came to collect his order. She remembers because they didn't have his usual bread and she apologised and he just grunted. As he left the shop she made a comment to this man. She doesn't remember what."

"Why short and ugly?"

"He was not much over five foot. She could only just see him above the glass of the counter, and ugly as in not handsome. She was a pretty young thing and she just thought him ugly. Nothing more."

"Anything else?"

"Here's the interesting bit. The café across the street; a waiter says he served a man with the same description who asked a question about the menswear shop. Thought nothing of it until I asked if he'd seen anybody hanging around."

"So we have a man of indeterminate age, short and ugly, who has been in the vicinity of the deceased. It's something at least. Well done Geoff, keep working the Marylebone area."

"Ben, I want you to get from London Underground all the CCTV footage of Balham Station. Let's assume he commutes by tube and it's a direct line to Warren Street, which is close to Marylebone Lane. Tell them we're looking to spot Michaels and anybody regularly following over, say, the previous few days to the murder. Check how long they archive their tapes. This is going to be laborious but crucial." Ben groaned inwardly. He was the newest member of the team and had only recently been transferred. He was keen to progress and watching tapes was not his idea of fun.

"Dick, what's turned up locally?" Strachan was impressed with Dick Williamson. He was a real pro and if he could fix it he wanted him transferred permanently.

"Boss, I think we've hit lucky. A number of neighbours have noticed a man that fits Geoff's description, at least the short bit and bomber jacket; he'd been hanging around the end of the street and as far as those who saw him could tell it was about the time Michaels came home. Nobody can ID him because it was either dusk or he was too far away."

"How many times and who?"

"It's in the log on the table." Strachan picked it up and scanned through it. At least three people had noticed and all said the man had now stopped coming.

"Good work all of you. Now I have something to tell you. This is not; repeat not to be talked about outside this room. Everybody understand?"

Nods from all his team. "Yesterday I had a call from a crime reporter saying his newspaper had received a message. It was in the form of a cut out pasted note with the words: 'Ask the police why the dead man in Balham had a broken thumb.'

The atmosphere in the room changed. They all knew now this was a crime where the killer wanted ownership of what he'd done. Possibly he wanted this to be published. There were murmurs but everyone was waiting for Strachan. "Obviously for the moment we are not saying we have this message and the press will play ball for a few days, but eventually it will break and then we'll be inundated with people coughing they did it. Any questions?"

Strangely no one asked. "Well that's a first," Strachan said smiling, "let's get back out there and see what else we can turn up. Searches of the area have not found the murder weapon and so far the footprint is of no use until we find the killer."

"Sir," it was Dick, "We believe Michaels has no living relatives, but perhaps this is a grudge killing by someone, or someone's relative who has had an argument or been disadvantaged by him at some stage. There are a lot of boxes in his loft we've yet to go through. Maybe in there is some link?"

"Another job, Dick. Take someone with you and bring it all here. Let's all see what his past contains. Thanks, see you all tomorrow morning to see what we've got. Instinct tells me Ben's job here is going to be crucial. The tapes will take you some time. See if they will release them so we can do it here."

Strachan walked out of the squad room and now he could hear the babble of talk amongst his team.

***

Jamie's buzz from what he had done was waning. What he craved more than anything was to read all about it in the newspapers. Was this a conspiracy? All there had been was the initial report. A week had passed since Frank had died and there had been no publicity following his note to the Daily Mail. He was tempted to send some other message but the same thing might happen, nothing. The television had been on all the time and all the news bulletins, local and national, failed to give further coverage. He was in the kitchen making a sandwich and suddenly there it was on the 'six o'clock news'. A policeman, not the one he had seen on the original bulletin, was being interviewed in a TV studio. Jamie had missed the introduction but turned up the volume. The credits stated the man was Detective Inspector George Strachan.

".... the death of Frank Michaels. There had been no developments in this case until an anonymous note was received some days ago about a particular aspect of this crime. I am not in a position to say what that was; to do so would prejudice the investigation. I regret at this stage there are no further leads except to say that evidence found at the scene of the crime will prove valuable in this case. I am taking this moment to bring to the public's attention that a ruthless killer is at large and there is a possibility this crime is not an isolated one. What is unclear to us at this stage is the motive. The victim appears to be a harmless man in his sixties who had been going about his business in a set routine for many years. He has no known relatives and although he worked as a tailor in London he had no work colleagues or friends. What we believe is that the killer may have been known to him, as there was no forced entry. That is all I am in a position to say at the moment."

A voice from the reporters much louder than the others shouted, "Why can't you tell us what was in the note?"

"I'm sorry but to divulge that would complicate the whole investigation."

"Was the note sent to you or the press?"

"I'm sorry, I can't comment. That's all. Thank you for coming."

The next day's local paper was splashed with the headline: 'Police no nearer solving Balham murder'. Jamie smiled. What could he do to speed up the process? He toyed with the idea of phoning the local paper and telling them about the broken thumb. He thought about this long and hard but what was the point? It was as though he wanted to set the police chasing him. No, he might have made a big mistake with the note to the press. He would wait and see what other developments occurred.

***

The three boxes containing the sum of Frank Michaels' life were placed on a table in the squad room. There was a notice placed on the box requiring gloves to be worn when touching the boxes or their contents. For the last few hours Dick Williamson had been leafing through photographs and correspondence. Most of the papers in the first box were old bank statements that he dreaded being asked to go through. He concentrated on the photos. There was not much. A whole batch appeared to relate to his chain of shops when he had been successful. Many pictures were with celebrities of the day for whom he had made clothes. Frank Michaels must have had a good business and it might prove necessary to look into what had led to such a decline. The second box was family and friends. There were pictures mainly in the early seventies, some with a pretty woman taken by the seaside. Dick had no idea where and the name on the back did not say where, but it did give a name, Carol.

Dick had no idea who Carol might be but as she was the only person to have more than one photo in the box, he decided to see if any letters and correspondence might throw any light on her relationship with the Michaels. He waded through papers, none of which he learned anything from until he saw an envelope that was sealed. All other letters were opened but this envelope stood out. It had a Central London postmark and was addressed to Frank at his shop in Marylebone. Dick carefully slit the envelope, wondering whether he should do so or whether he should show it first to Strachan. It could be something, more likely it was nothing. He reached in with tweezers and pulled out the letter and started to read. He knew immediately the letter might be crucial. He read it twice and then walked along to Strachan's office.

"Think we might have something here. He placed the photo and letter on his desk. Strachan peered down. "Who's she?"

"Carol. That's all it says on the back but the letter says more."

Strachan read it out loud:

> *"My dearest Frank. I know you don't want to know me after I became pregnant and I accept I can't force you. Just so you know your son was born a week ago and I've called him James. I always liked that name.*

> *There is no question, you are his father and I felt you ought to know and if you want to play a part in his life then that's your right. For my part I don't care. He is such a beautiful baby. If you do not contact me within one month of this letter then you will have nothing to do with him ever. I will be moving and I shall not be telling you where?"*

Strachan looked up. "What do you think Dick? Could this killing be connected? Has the son sought him out and killed him? Seems a bit extreme if he did."

"How do you want to proceed?"

"Keep looking through the files. Bag these as evidence for the moment; we have nothing else and have forensics check the envelope seal for DNA. We might be able to trace the mother or James from it. Let's not get side-lined by it. Do you know how Ben's getting on with the tapes?"

"No idea."

"Have this at the briefing tomorrow plus anything else you find. Tell Ben to ring me. Good work."

"Boss, phone." It was Gemma.

"Not now Gemma. Tell them I'll ring back."

"I think you'll want to take this. It's Jim from the Mail."

"Put it through to my office."

"Hi Jim, what gives?" He was trying to be jocular but feared the worst.

"Sorry George but my editor is going with the story. He can't wait and thinks we may lose out when everybody gets the story."

"So you are going to say what was in the note. Any room for negotiation?"

"None. The story is on the wire and I've faxed you a copy."

"Thanks for that, at least I can prepare. I was surprised you held off so long. You still get the first interview personally as promised. I'll ring you later when I see what the fall out on this is." He put down the phone not wanting any further discussion and rang the boss to give him the news.

"Look George get a statement prepared and let me see it. I think at this stage I don't want anybody in front of the cameras."

"I'll get on it straight away."

"Have you promised Jim anything? My view all bets are off as they're breaking the story."

"I've said he'll get the first face to face. I need him. He's useful and he wouldn't have broken his word."

"OK. Send me the statement as soon as you can."

The line went dead, leaving George thinking about the next step. What did he want to come out of this? He wasn't sure whilst they were still searching the CCTV tapes and the boxes.

Dick knocked and walked in. "I've searched the records and there is no record of Michael's having a legitimate son."

"What about children registered as James or Jamie in the London area around the time of the postmark on that letter?"

"Blimey Sir. That could take a while. I'll need help, can searches be speeded up?"

"Call Smith in Admin. He's a wiz. He'll know."

Dick left the room and George felt although they had made big strides he had nothing he wanted to share with the media. Gemma brought in a fax from the Mail. He read the article and it was not as bad as it could have been. What it would do was bring every crank in the City out of his hole in the ground claiming to be the killer. All this would do is increase the workload, as each individual would have to be ruled in or out.

The next day he grabbed the newspaper from his wife as they sat at breakfast. The article was tucked inside which was a bonus and reflected that the Mail only wanted to be first, not to ratchet the story higher.

"That's a relief," he said to Madge who only vaguely knew what he was talking about. Of much more concern to her was what she was to wear at Sam's lunch party.

"Have you asked Sam what the dress code is?"

"Have I what?" he said mildly irritated.

"Asked Sam what I should wear."

"Sam said she would ring you. Ask her then. I've got to go. Busy day today. Bye love." He kissed her forehead as he passed and was gone before she could ask him anything else.

***

Jamie read the papers that morning as usual and nearly missed the piece in the Mail. He was really angry. Angry that nobody yet knew the details of Frank Michaels' murder. What could he do about it? To send another note might do nothing but put him at risk of being traced and why was it so important anyway for it to be known anyway?

Deep down he knew his anger was he'd been robbed of the absolute confirmation, from the horse's mouth that Frank Michaels was his father. Somehow it robbed him of the satisfaction he wanted from having exacted his revenge, even if it had gone further than he'd planned. Then again what exactly did he think he was going to do having attacked Frank? He could hardly say goodbye and walk out of the house and expect to get away with it. Such was his desire to fight back against those who had done him wrong he actually hadn't thought it through carefully at all.

Now he was a killer and with nothing to show for it. Perhaps he would do it again. Yes maybe he could get revenge on someone else who he hated. Then somehow he might link the two killings, but how?

This was a crazy notion and he felt stupid at the thought he could get away with it. Anyway did he hate anyone enough to take that risk? He put the notion out of his mind and sat at the computer to look up some information on the web. He would decide later when he saw what other media developments occurred on the killing.

He picked up the newspapers from the convenience store. They must have wondered why he was now out every day, in an out of the store both during the day and at night. The headlines of the local paper shouted out him. 'Killer still loose. Police following leads.'

When he read the piece it showed since the contents of the note had been published the police had been inundated with cranks claiming to have committed the crime or have personal knowledge of it. The police were chasing leads that led nowhere but tied up their precious time. Jamie fumed but had no idea what to do. He wanted somehow to take ownership of what he'd done but that would be suicide. He would be caught.

He walked home and sat thinking about the whole mess. Mess it might be but he had no regrets at what he'd done. It was like a release and having done it he was being denied 'bragging rights'.

***

Jamie logged on to the web. Other than TV, the web was his favourite pastime. He was well read and always acquisitive for knowledge. His focus at present was the crime websites. First he loved to visit Wikipedia. It was possible to find out about almost everything. He typed in 'crime' and started to read. He clicked on 'murder' and it confirmed what he had done amounted to murder. He typed 'murderers' and was staggered to find a site called 'murders database' which listed killers in Britain, USA and most other major countries. He clicked on Ronnie and Reggie Kray and it listed their reign of terror and those they had killed, then James Hanratty, the A6 Killer in 1961, who had shot a man and her lover for no known motive. He could not believe the amount of information freely available. He looked at the entries for serial killers Donald Neilson and Peter Sutcliffe and looked at some of the American serial killers. An idea was beginning to form in his head, if he were to kill someone else; he would need to make the killing identifiable with the murder of his father. Yes, his father, it had a nice ring about it. His father had abandoned him, left his mother to become a prostitute to bring him up and now he was dead. Revenge was not yet sweet, but it was getting closer.

He had killed once although he hadn't gone out with that intention. It just turned out that way and the fact he felt no guilt wasn't bothering him; quite the reverse. The elation he had felt at fighting back seemed to empower him; but was he prepared to do it again and if so who would be his second victim?

Reading about murderers was fascinating him. He decided to examine serial killers in some depth. He needed to find out if the information provided would provide an insight into how they went about their work. Was it opportunistic or highly planned? Were they unhinged or intelligent ruthless people? Did they truly know what they were doing or were they overtaken by some primeval urge? Did they remain happy with their actions or did they lapse into deep remorse? Most of all did they have the notion they would be caught or were they above and beyond the law?

During this process he convinced himself that he would have to be stupid to follow this line of thought. He was no killer. He couldn't legislate for Frank's heart attack but Jamie felt sure Frank knew that his past had caught up with him. He just had no idea what would happen to him and then he died. 'So be it' thought Jamie, 'I can't put the clock back, but I need to lay more ghosts from the past'.

There was one glaringly obvious candidate, his form teacher at school, Mr Jacobson, he of the heavy hand slapping the back of his head. Jacobson had taken delight in humiliating Jamie in class for no reason in particular; how unfair he thought when he had been one of the brightest until his mother's cancer. Despite that Jacobson continued to punish him. Jacobson had not bothered to find out why Jamie's performance was suffering; he called himself a teacher. More like he was taking it out on Jamie for all the suffering of the entire Jewish nation. Yes, Jacobson could be next for a visit.

He had not intended to kill his father. Surely all killers get caught in the end. He had the greatest chance if he kept a low profile. He put the thought of further revenge out of his mind.

Jamie's Internet searching became compulsive. The next day he never left home. He was on the web all day. His interest in serial killers had led him to one of the most notorious in America. Ted Bundy, a good-looking young man who killed 37 women in five years from 1973. His motives were sex. He frequently feigned injury with an arm in a sling or a fake cast to gain the trust of his victims. All were young students or nurses and on occasions he had killed the next victim before a week had passed. His notoriety was heightened as a result of his escape during a trial in 1977 during which he killed again. Sentenced to death he gave an interview on the eve of his execution admitting to 37 killings, some victims were never found in the wilds of the mountains of Washington State, Utah and Colorado.

Jamie was disgusted when he read that Bundy would revisit the corpses until they had finally decomposed.

His search of British murderers led him to James Hanratty, 'The A6 Killer' notorious for the murder of a man and the sexual assault on his lover in 1961. It appeared a motiveless killing and reports later suggested his conviction was an error. The description given by the woman did not match that of Hanratty but he was convicted and sentenced to hang. This took place in 1962 and a later campaign for a pardon led to his body being exhumed. DNA tests gave a 2.5 million to one possibility he didn't do it but that was insufficient for a posthumous pardon. Jamie was fascinated.

He went out for a walk to clear his head. The blossom on the street trees had faded and it was now light until well after eight o' clock. Nevertheless he carried his new 'Maglite' torch with him. It had served him well as he had emerged from his forced hibernation of the last year or so. It was the end of that day when he had made a momentous decision. He would seek more revenge. "Jacobson; are you still alive and how will I find you?"

A woman had been passing him and turned, wondering what he must have been saying to himself. Jamie was oblivious, locked in his little world. He didn't even see the gang hanging on the corner of the street until it was too late. Were these the thugs who had beaten him up? If they were, what would he do if they recognised him? Perhaps he should thank them for waking him from his long slumber. It was too late to take avoiding action. That would increase their interest so he walked past with as much confidence as he could muster. They paid him no attention whatsoever.

Then he was free and out into safety. It occurred to him timidity must excite the interest of a gang and to walk past normally was definitely the safest option. Maybe, but he would take a different route back home to be sure.

***

Strachan picked up the phone. It had been ringing for a few minutes and Gemma had not picked it up. "Strachan."

"It's Jim. What's the latest on the Balham murder? My boss is still looking for a lead bearing in mind we played ball on not publishing straight away."

"Played ball! Against our wishes you published. Despite what I may have promised all bets are off. You get what everyone else gets and when they get it." Strachan said it for maximum effect. He had no intention of breaking his word. He needed Jim from time to time; the two had worked together but the scores were even.

"Hang on, you promised."

"Did I? Well now I'm thinking of breaking that promise." He kept up the pretence as long as he could; he didn't want a falling out. "Only kidding."

"Bastard."

"Still nothing to say publicly. We've no firm knowledge of anybody who might be involved," he lied, "but we do think someone had been hanging around both the house and the shop."

"What does that mean? Has somebody been identified?"

"No, but we are now looking at CCTV tapes at the stations where the victim caught the tube to see what we find. I should be making a statement tomorrow and you will be invited. I'll talk to you separately afterwards."

"Fair enough."

"Now stop bothering me."

"Cheers."

Strachan put down the receiver. He was going out on a limb saying he would talk to Jim separately; he'd done it before but he had a feeling about this case. Instinct told him this might not be a one off murder. Despite the pathology report telling him Michaels died from heart failure, it would take a pretty deranged person then to stab him repeatedly when dead.

***

Sam heard the door open and the man of her life breezed in. He was carrying flowers.

"What have you done wrong?" She challenged him; flowers were not an Eddie thing.

"Nothing. Can't a bloke buy the woman of his dreams flowers?"

"There is a first time I suppose," Sam said not wanting to spoil his moment, "they're lovely. I'll get a vase."

"Thought you deserved flowers. I've been working late such a lot and you've not been out, except to see George. Anyway I thought they would brighten up the place for the party."

"You are a sweetie, I do love you so." She snuggled into his arms and kissed him passionately.

"Mmm. Eat first or sex. It's your choice."

"Don't be silly." The twins had screeched into the hall and wanted a cuddle. Sam could hear Mark squealing for attention.

"Guess it'll have to be later then." He dashed into the playroom to gather Mark into his arms for a hug.

This was a scene that Sam never tired of watching, her contentment evident for anyone who might have been watching.

***

Jamie had made his decision. He couldn't justify why but he had to confront Jacobson. He had to exorcise the demons of his terrible end at school. He was the outstanding candidate. Punishment in schools was restricted but that never bothered Jacobson. Often he would be harsher if nobody else could see but the mental torture of being humiliated in front of the class was just as bad. One day his mother wanted to know why his knuckles were caked with blood. He told her he'd scuffed his hand against a wall whilst playing football in the playground. That seemed to placate her; the truth was somewhat different.

Jacobson had kept Jamie behind after class; ostensibly to discuss some aspect of his homework. In truth he had wanted to exert his power over Jamie. He had an old classroom pointer in his desk and he had whacked Jamie's hand with it. Jamie had no real idea why. He felt there was little to be gained by complaining; it would only make matters worse.

Jamie looked on the web for the telephone number for his old school and found it. He was surprised; it was an old school when he was there and he felt sure it would've been knocked down to make way for a supermarket or housing development. He dialled the number. It rang for a long while before someone answered.

"Secretary's office."

This confused him. He expected to go through a switchboard. "Hello. I hope you can help me. I'm trying to locate a Mr Jacobson who was a teacher 25 years ago at your school."

"I knew Mr Jacobson, but he retired some years ago, lives in Hatfield I think. We're not allowed to give out information on ex-employees. I'm sorry I can't help you."

"Thanks anyway." Jamie put the phone down. It was a start, but not much to go on. He looked at the Internet phone directories to identify everyone in Hatfield with the name Jacobson and decided to ring each one with a story, he hadn't decided yet what that would be, and then see if he could get any identification of his old teacher.

He went back on line and typed in Jacobson and Hatfield and to his great surprise up popped more than a dozen telephone numbers and addresses. "How easy was that?"

He jotted down all the addresses and numbers and sat back thinking what he might say when he rang. He felt it dangerous to admit to knowing the man from the past and certainly he did not want to give his name. He decided to tell them they were winners of a competition and see how it went from there. He might even recognise the twang of Jacobson's eastern European background.

He sat looking at the phone and then got scared. What if in a search they look at my phone records and find that I contacted him? What was the alternative? He could hardly go to a pay phone to make such a call. It would not be believable. "Nothing for it, it's a risk I'll just have to take."

He rang the first number. In front of him was a piece of paper with his spiel written on it. The phone rang for a short while and a lady answered.

"Good afternoon, can I speak to Mr Jacobson please?"

"Sorry, I'm Mrs Jacobson but there is no Mr Jacobson."

"I'm sorry to have bothered you." Jamie put down the phone quickly. Then he was annoyed with himself. He hadn't ruled out that number; it was just possible there had been a Mr Jacobson but he might have died. If he drew a blank with the other calls he might have to call again. At least he could enquire whether there had been a Mr Jacobson and whether he had been a teacher. It would then be a perfectly innocent conversation.

He rang a succession of numbers all of which remained unanswered or defaulted to an answer phone. He made notes against each number. He had six to go when he hit lucky.

"Hello, may I speak to Mr Jacobson please?"

"That's me but who are you?"

The voice was unmistakeable. It brought memories flooding back to Jamie from his childhood. He could see Jacobson's Jewish features even now. He imagined him with a stoop and a dishevelled appearance. Never one of nature's smartest, he thought. "Mr Jacobson, we need to identify you. You have won a prize of a new kitchen and we would like to talk to you about your wishes."

"Bugger off." The phone went dead but Jamie was elated. Ten calls and he now knew that Jacobson was alive and where he lived.

Jamie was so excited that he felt he had achieved enough today and turned on the TV to watch 'Countdown'. This was not a regular occurrence but there was precious little of interest on in the late afternoon. He got a beer out of the fridge and sat down to contemplate his next move. He would look at 'Google map' to locate his house and go out to Hatfield on the train for a recce. He would go tomorrow whilst he felt so positive. He was beginning to feel his confidence might be misplaced, after all when he'd gone to confront his father he had no plan to kill him. That was the outcome but it had happened by accident. He had no intention of killing Jacobson but what might happen if this got out of control?

The next day he headed for Kings Cross and caught a train out to Hatfield. It was a very long time since he had been out of London and he watched the countryside slip by as the train sped quickly towards his possible meeting with a man he actually hated more than his father. As the train pulled in to Hatfield station he could just see the top of the historic Elizabethan Hatfield House. He would have no time to visit but thought it would be interesting to see the grand palace where "Good Queen Bess" had lived; but that would have to wait. He would have quite a walk according to his map. He had no idea whether buses went nearby or not and he certainly was not going to take a taxi. It was at least a mile and a half before he turned into the road he was looking for. The houses were small and box like; nothing like the Victorian houses around Tooting. He walked down and identified Jacobson's house.

He had no idea what to do next so he went to the end of the street where there was a kid's playground and benches to sit on. This was on the edge of a large wooded park. A single man sitting by the playground might be suspicious so he walked past and round the block again, looking to see signs of life in the house. He crossed to the other side of the street and walked around the corner. There was no way he could wait in broad daylight so he went to a phone box down the next road. It looked as though it had been vandalised but it was actually working. He rang Jacobson's number but there was no answer. He walked back to town and wandered around aimlessly before deciding to head for home. He had achieved little; but at least he knew where Jacobson lived. He arrived home tired and slightly in awe of the task he had now set himself.

Chapter 16

Enrico Suarez was not a wanted man; but Bill Millichip was. Bill's contact had said there was a permanent watch for him at all ports and airports. It had led him to travel as a Spanish tourist, but he had found no difficulty getting into the country. His Spanish passport was top quality; but then so were all his other passports. Even so he had worried as he walked through passport control at Leeds Bradford airport along with tourists returning from Spain but nobody had even questioned him.

He walked outside into the warm sunshine of late May. There was nobody to meet him and he was annoyed. He expected to be looked after. Others had lived well off him and people should be there when he needed them. After a few minutes a black Mercedes pulled into the taxi lane and stopped opposite Bill. The door swung open.

"Thought you'd forgotten."

"Can't park here and didn't want to draw attention to ourselves." Bill slid into the back seat and his old friend Garry was already sitting there. He had an expensive suit and dark glasses. 'Archetypal hood' thought Bill and that's exactly what he was. He had been Bill's fixer, except when he had needed him in Peru he had gone missing. 'Must talk to him about that', he thought.

The car moved off at a measured pace. "We have to be careful. Don't want to draw attention to ourselves."

"A black Mercedes, with darkened windows? You're joking."

"Could have come in a clapped out Mondeo if that's more to your liking."

"Whatever. Where are we going?"

"Farmhouse in Cheshire. Very secluded. Nobody pays us any attention. Thousands of top motors all over the area; footballers' paradise. We run it as an exclusive Limo car hire and taxi service; sort of legit. That's why you are sitting in this Merc now."

"How many of the team left?"

"None. You'll see how we run it. Virtually everything's cash and we convert it to euros and every so often drive down to Spain and deposit cash into your account. What's your story?"

"When I finally got to Buenos Aires I only just escaped being arrested. They were waiting for me but my men set fire to a car to create a diversion and I got away. I've had to move around all the time for a while but then they seemed to stop chasing me. Settled at the family farm in Argentina. They didn't seem too bothered. There's still a few old Nazis living safely in the country. Luckily I had good people. Loyal. They looked after me. Everything's closed down in Peru. The authorities have closed all the coca routes and the police force is much more honest."

"Why did you come back? It's risky."

Bill looked at the back of the driver's head. "He alright? Can we talk?"

"My youngest brother. He's my fixer, like I was yours. Die for the cause- hey John?"

"Hope not."

"So why back now?"

"Scores to settle. Anyway I got arrested when I went to Buenos Aires to see some doctors. So much for all that loyalty crap. There's always someone who'll sell you for enough dosh."

"So I ask again. Why? You're lucky you're free?"

"So are you."

"Maybe, but I wasn't there when you killed what's his name; the one who shot Julia..."

"Lucky old you."

"….and I didn't set fire to the barn with that copper and her boyfriend in it."

"So what you're saying is that I should just forget that Sam… what's her name, should just get away with ruining my business and my life."

"So what do you want to do?"

"We are going to finish the job. Sam Jones is dead meat."

"What? You must be barmy. Do you know she got a medal for what she did and you want to kill her? Not with our help."

"You'll do as you're told."

"Sod off. We've moved on. I have a legit business and we're straight. You've got enough money to live comfortably, why put it at risk?"

"You owe me, Garry. This is payback time. Either you help me or…"

"Or what? What you going to do about it? You're lucky we still look out for you. By rights after what you did we should have cleared off. Everyone else scarpered. Heard nothing from them since. Do you know how much police activity there was, all looking for you? You lost all the properties and I had to start again. If it had been someone else I'd have gone too. As it was I owed you; but that's repaid. I'm not doing anything that puts what we've achieved for you at risk.

Bill sat thinking about his next move. "We'll talk about it later."

"The answer will be the same."

The rest of the journey passed in silence but the mood in the car was menacing.

Strachan's phone rang. It was Juan Ramos.

"Bill Millichip is definitely back. It was a false alarm before. Immigration at Leeds Bradford reported him coming in. He was on a Spanish passport and was not clocked."

"Why not? Do we know where he is now?"

"No."

"Sod it. We'll have to alert Sam and Eddie. Step up the surveillance on them."

"Okay but what do we want to do about finding Millichip?"

"Does he have any remaining mates? Anyone we can watch?"

"Not as far as we know. They all headed for the hills but I'll check the files and get back to you."

***

The Merc turned into the driveway of what at first sight looked like a posh farm. The driveway was lined with trees and as soon as they were half way along Bill turned and looked behind. The place was virtually invisible from the road. The car pulled up by a set of open farm buildings in which were parked a number of limos including a long pink Cadillac.

"This is the business I've built up and don't want to put at risk. You live off half the income but it's all in my name. If you want to go on some shooting spree then you're on your own."

"You don't want me for an enemy Garry. Think hard before answering. Are you going to help me or not?"

"You thick or something? What in 'no' don't you understand? I said 'no' and I meant 'no'."

Garry didn't see the elbow that broke his nose. John turned but caught Bill's fist on the side of his chin and he slumped against the wheel and the car careered into the pink Cadillac. John's face was saved further damage by the air bag that exploded on impact. Garry may have had a broken nose but he was quick to regain himself and he lunged at Bill. Bill was hampered by the airbag that had stopped him crashing into the front seat. Garry wasn't so lucky. The impact sent him crashing into the headrest. The car was now stopped. The horn was blaring.

Bill looked at Garry; he was motionless but breathing with difficulty, choking on his own blood. John was now looking to get out of the car but Bill lent over the seat and grabbed his head and jerked it sharply. John's neck snapped. Bill got out of the car and lent in to check John was dead. He reached inside his jacket and pulled out a gun. He poked the gun over the back of the seat and shot Garry through the forehead. He slumped forward still in his seat belt. Bill moved to the house quickly before anyone came out to see what had happened. He watched the doors and windows. It seemed as though nobody was there. He walked across and the door was locked, perhaps it was empty.

He broke a window and luckily no alarm sounded. He climbed into the kitchen and took stock. It was old; stone floors and an Aga. What he wanted was a set of keys to a car. He had no intention of hanging around. He found a rack on the wall with keys for five cars. They had labels. He ignored the pink Cadillac and then found keys for a Range Rover. He picked them off the hook and walked out to the yard. The Merc was still smoking. Steam from the radiator was hissing from the crumpled bonnet. He saw the Range Rover and opened it up and put the key in and started it up. It had a tank almost full so this was the one he would take. He went back in the house and searched for money lying around. It didn't take him long. In an old tin he found a roll of notes. It looked about £500 so he grabbed it and a bottle of water from the fridge and left the house.

He backed out the Range Rover and started down the drive. Then he remembered his bag in the Merc. He reversed and retrieved it. He looked at Garry, his smashed up face and a neat hole in his forehead. He felt odd; Garry had been his last and only link in England; now he was on his own. There were others that owed him. Where they had disappeared to he had no idea and now there was nobody to ask. He would have to think about that another time. Now he needed to get out of this place before Garry's mates turned up to find what had happened. He climbed back into the Range Rover and set out for London. He had scores to settle and quickly.

***

"Sam, I thought you better know that George rang. He says Bill Millichip is definitely back. He came through Leeds Bradford Airport yesterday on a false passport and they don't know where he is now." Eddie had a way of dealing with serious matters in a very calm and collected way. It was good but it irritated Sam.

"Bugger."

"They're putting more surveillance on the house so we'll be okay."

"I know but it just means we're virtual prisoners," Sam said disappointed the news they had been hanging over them for nearly four years was now confirmed, "and just when life is so perfect."

"And perfect it will remain," Eddie said, not believing it.

"Does George want to talk to me?"

"Yes, but not immediately. He's got some activity on the Balham case. He'll ring."

Eddie walked out of the kitchen. That was it, message given and on with business. She wondered how he could deal with such an important issue in such a matter-of-fact way.

***

Strachan was feeling uncomfortable. The Chief was questioning him about the Balham murder. He had been catching flak from above.

"If we don't get lucky soon we'll have a real problem upstairs. What's the latest on the CCTV footage?"

"I haven't had the detailed report yet but the team have found on consecutive days a young man following Michaels at a reasonable distance through Balham station. The positioning of the cameras has not allowed an ID but it is a bit odd on two consecutive nights the same two people get off the same train."

"Could be coincidence. Michaels was a creature of habit; same train most nights, perhaps this man was the same. Any luck with Warren Street?"

"Not yet but we're getting images of the man to show to the sandwich shop and the waiter across the road. I'm sending an artist along to see if we can construct an image from their descriptions."

"OK. Keep me posted. We need a break and quickly."

***

Jamie set off for Hatfield. He had no clear idea of what would happen. This would not be as easy as following his father to find the right moment. The distance alone made it more difficult. He really had no clue about the surrounding area or how he would confront Jacobson.

It was bright and warm as he left the station. He set out for Jacobson's house with a strangely detached feeling. There now seemed no pressure. Before he had been desperate to fight back, gain revenge for wrongs done to him. He could take that as closure but the buzz he'd got from attacking his father was intoxicating. He wanted more. He would definitely play this by ear. The annoying thing was he would be making this long journey, possibly frequently, until the right opportunity arose. It could take ages before the moment presented itself, if at all.

So he might have to be opportunistic, take his chance quickly when it presented itself. And this is how it turned out that day, but there was no sight of Jacobson; he might even have been away from Hatfield.

Two more visits were the same, nothing. Nothing happening was the worst thing for Jamie. He had the bit between his teeth and was surprised to find he was getting impatient. From feeling nonchalant, he'd got his initial revenge. He hadn't planned to murder his father, but he now needed to finish what he had started. How could his life have changed so dramatically and so quickly? He would need to do something within the next couple of visits or call it a day, but it was chipping away at his logic. Logic said he should quit and not put himself at risk. Jamie was fighting to erase logical thought from his mind. He wanted the next thrill, whatever the consequence.

Chapter 17

Jamie's frustration was mounting. He hadn't actually seen Jacobson yet. He had no picture in his mind of what he might look like now. He must have retired five or more years ago so he would definitely look really old; he had looked old when Jamie last saw him; that day all those years ago when he walked out of school and never looked back.

Jamie wondered how he could get to see him. He could ring and call round; confront him at the door as he did his father. The trouble with that idea was it was now light late into the evening and shrubs did not protect the front door of his house, the neighbours would have an uninterrupted view of their meeting. No, he had to wait his moment even if that took some time. It was on his sixth visit to Hatfield he hit lucky. He actually saw Jacobson in a street walking back from the town centre and instantly recognised him. He was certain. It was as though he had grown old in exactly the features he always had. He followed him to his house. Jacobson walked to his door and went inside. Jamie pondered what to do next. He had a positive identification; this was his teacher. This was the man who had made his life a misery at school. He had now decided just to confront him on the doorstep, to talk to him and ask why he had been so unfair in his treatment of him. Then he wanted in some way to humiliate Jacobson but in what way he was unsure.

Then suddenly Jacobson came out of his house and turned towards the park away to the right, Jamie had seen it on his earlier visits. Jacobson was carrying a walking stick, but Jamie had not noticed him carrying it when he went inside. Jamie kept his distance. His heart was pounding.

Strangely, he again felt ill-prepared. If he were to confront him today he would have to think quickly on his feet when the time came. Jacobson crossed into the park and headed for the wooded area over to the left. Jamie tracked him but entered the wood a little further on.

He still had sight of him and he moved as quietly as he could. Suddenly he saw Jacobson turn round. Perhaps he knew he was being followed but Jamie could see he was looking behind him and not to where Jamie was crouching. Jamie stayed hidden for a few minutes and then heard a noise. He stood up slowly and Jacobson was standing directly in front of him.

"What are you doing? You're following me."

Jamie had no idea what to say. It was as though he had been caught red handed and he felt foolish. "I wasn't," he blurted.

Jacobson suddenly lunged forward with alarming speed with his cane raised. Jamie ducked as he swung it close to his head. Then Jamie's anger flared and he charged at Jacobson and knocked him over. Jamie quickly had the upper hand and wrenched the cane free. Jamie's heart was pounding. He was almost on the verge of losing control and lashing out at the old man. His father's face flashed before his eyes and he stopped. What was the point of losing control again and hurting this man? Had he really intended to hurt his father physically, or it was just the way it had turned out? What he did want was for Jacobson to know the harm he had caused to Jamie's life.

"I don't want to hurt you. Do you have any idea who I am?" Jamie realised the futility of his question. Twenty years had passed since he had last seen his old teacher.

He thought he saw a flicker of recognition but Jacobson said nothing.

He realised the total futility of what he was doing. He had wanted revenge, but why. That would be looking back and what would it achieve? What his earlier beating had done was to release him from his imprisonment. In an instant he made his decision and dropped Jacobson's cane, turned and walked away out of the wood.

He heard Jacobson shout but he wasn't about to turn round. His decision was made and he felt more in control of his life for the first time since his mother had died.

Within minutes he was out of the wood. He could no longer hear Jacobson shouting after him. He walked rather than ran. It was still better he not draw attention to himself so he walked back along a road which he assumed would take him back towards the town centre and back to Hatfield station. Within thirty minutes he was on a train back home.

It seemed an endless journey but at last he was home. He flopped into his favourite chair.

Now he had to hope that Jacobson had not recognised him. But then again he had committed no crime. Jacobson had raised his cane to him. Maybe Jacobson would not report the encounter. One thing he had decided was he was not looking back any more. The future was what mattered. This whole exercise had been about freeing himself from the imprisonment bullying had brought about all these years.

Somehow this seemed significant despite the fact he had actually killed his father. He had no idea whether he would get caught. Modern forensics increased the likelihood he would and this would be more likely if they ever make the link between him and his father. What could he do? He could go on the run; he had enough money to leave the country but that might draw even more attention to himself. He decided to ensure no incriminating evidence was in the flat and he would set about destroying all his mother's papers, including the various photos of Frank.

He sat down to put the whole day in perspective. Had he covered his tracks? He had bought his tickets with cash; he had tried as far as he could to be inconspicuous, although hanging around the vicinity of Jacobson's home had been a big risk.

He went to the computer and clicked on the web. He typed in 'DNA'. Up came the Wikipedia site and he scrolled down to 'profiling'. It showed how the police could gather DNA from anyone arrested and how valuable this had been for forensic evidence. He scrolled further to see how DNA was gathered; it listed blood, saliva, semen, skin and hair. He wondered whether the struggles with his father and Jacobson would have left any of his own saliva, skin or hair as incriminating evidence.

He also looked at 'criminal investigations' and decided it had been a mistake not to get rid of his trainers when he had thrown everything else in the back of the rubbish truck. He would destroy all the clothes he had worn and his favourite trainers.

He cleared all files off his laptop, deleted his Internet history and emptied his recycle bin. Whether this was sufficient he had no idea. He would have no clothes left from that night so as far as he could tell he would remove all links with his father and Jacobson.

***

Jamie left home that evening with a carrier bag. He had worn his Nike trainers both at his father's house and in Hatfield. They were a popular design and there could be thousands around but he had slashed the soles with a sharp knife hoping to obscure any particular marks that if they were found might identify them as having been worn at both places. Whether it would make a difference he had no idea but it made him feel better. He had even washed them before he wrapped them around in an old towel and tied the whole bundle with string. If he was unable to burn them he would have to throw them in the canal or a river but he had to be sure they would not resurface. Burning was the preferred option but one which could draw attention to himself. He walked trying to think where the best place might be. He wanted to find a fire that was already alight and he could throw on his package without drawing attention to himself, but where would he find a fire at this time of year?

In the end he couldn't bring himself to find another canal or river and threw the shoes and bag in a commercial rubbish bin behind a parade of shops.

***

Strachan was reading the pathologists' detailed report of Frank Michaels' killing when his boss walked in.

"George I need to free up your time to concentrate on the Michael's murder, so I'm taking everything else off you except Michaels."

"Not Millichip. He's mine. It's personal, I want to keep on top of that myself."

Gilliard thought for a moment. "Ok but this takes priority. Have a watching brief; put Juan Ramos in day to day charge."

"I'm totally happy with him, but he's only seconded to us."

"I've asked him if he wants to stay with us and he's thinking about it. When I pointed out he might find it difficult to go back he asked in what capacity he could stay. If we give him some line authority it'll help him decide. I assume you'd have no objection."

"None whatsoever. We owe him big time over Sam."

"Pass Millichip to him but oversee it. I'll send a note round he's in charge reporting to you. Now you concentrate on this murder."

***

Sam was dying to know how Juan was getting on with his new girlfriend. She had liked Jayne Grayson when she met her at the party. The party had been such a great success. It was the first time she had ever entrusted catering to outsiders and they'd been brilliant. She kept out of the way and had real fun chatting to everyone. The surprise of the evening was a wonderful speech by George full of emotion but also very funny about her life in the police. Sam's mother had moist eyes when George referred to Sam's father who had shaped his own life so dramatically. Eddie had been brilliant. He was great with everyone and also kept the girls happy and Mum had Mark under firm control. Mark adored his grandmother and was always happy to be carried around the party. Mark was good with company at eye level but hated being left on the floor when people were around.

Sam had gone up to bed before everyone had left. The baby was letting her know she was over doing it and it was wonderful to wake up next morning to a clean house and no hangover. The same could not be said for Eddie who decided not to go to work the next day.

Sam dialled George's number and Gemma answered.

"Hi Sam, if you want George he's out. Juan is with him. Did you know Juan is in charge of your Millichip case?"

"No but that's great. I won't bother George on his mobile, just tell him I rang and it's not urgent. Is he likely to be able to do lunch next week?"

"He told me to keep his diary free but he usually makes an exception in your case."

"OK thanks." Sam hung up. She was now dying to know about the Balham case and why was Juan with him. Now Juan was in charge of the Millichip case it set her wondering where that thug was now. It was some weeks ago since he had landed back in England and he was obviously still a threat to her, Eddie and the kids.

She sat down with a coffee. She was uncomfortable. The baby was lying awkwardly and she could not sit in a low chair at all. She perched on a stool by the breakfast bar. The phone rang and it startled her. She picked it up but there was nobody there. She asked twice before hanging up. She wondered whether it was sinister but it could have been one of those annoying computer driven sales calls. It wasn't logical but as Bill Millichip was in her thinking she could not help making the connection.

The phone rang again. She picked up cautiously but did not speak.

"Are you there Sam?" It was George.

"Yes, I'm here George. What a coincidence I was thinking about you. Did you ring a few moments ago?"

"No. Why?"

"Oh nothing. The phone rang and no-one was there."

George noted it but said nothing. "Gemma said you rang. Can you come in? I need to review with Juan and you the Bill Millichip position. We'll have a sandwich and you can chat to Ruth again."

"Are lunches gone forever?"

"For the moment, but not forever. Anyway buying you lunch at the moment would be a waste. You and your food fads; I saw what you were eating at the party and your mum even spoke to me about it."

"Stop lecturing me."

"Are you coming on Wednesday or not?"

"I'll be there. Usual time?"

***

Jamie's life had been changed forever. Having broken free of the shackles of imprisonment in his own home he no longer felt so insecure walking outside although he was happier in daylight than at night. It was beginning to dawn on him his freedom may only have come at a terrible price. Ever since that moment when he attacked his father he could not bring himself to regret his actions. He had lost control when denied the certainty of hearing from Frank the very thing he wanted to know, but he did not regret his actions. Unless he was very lucky one day there would be a knock at the door and the police would be there to arrest him. All he could do was minimise the risk of it happening. If he went on the run that might draw attention to him so for the time being he was staying put and living as normally as possible.

He might buy a small motorbike; he felt it would give him much more freedom. He still had a licence for one and he could park it at the back of his apartment block. Apart from the helmet he couldn't be bothered with all the gear. He was only going to use it on sunny days anyway. Anyway that was a plan for later.

Chapter 18

Bill Millichip had tracked down Grieve. Grieve had been on 'his' payroll at Scotland Yard. It was he who had helped spirit Sam away from the hospital after the fire at the barn when Bill bungled his plan to kill Eddie and Sam. Grieve had served time for kidnapping Sam but was out on parole despite strong activity on the part of the police to prevent it.

He knew Grieve's patch around the Elephant & Castle and it hadn't taken him long to find him. Ginger hair was the real giveaway. He saw Grieve sitting at a table at the back of the pub and sat down next to him.

"What do you want? You mad or something? Half the worlds' coppers are looking for you."

"Shut up and listen. I need your help."

"You're joking. You're a bleeding head case and I'm not going near you."

Grieve never saw the fist slam into his face and he slumped onto the table. The barman started round the bar. He took one look at Bill's face and decided against it. The only other customers a flashily dressed woman and a man left quickly.

"Good thinking mate. Now be a good man and lock the door and there's a twenty in it for you."

The barman slid the bolt on the door and Bill gave him the note. He left to tidy up the cellar. Bill waited for Grieve to come round.

"Hit me again, it makes no difference. Being seen with you gets me dead or banged up again. From what I hear you've already croaked Garry and John. You must be barmy."

"What I am is angry. I need help and if you aren't giving it you are no use alive or dead. I'll be dead soon anyway so if you want yours now you can have it." Bill drew his gun and pointed at Grieve's head. Grieve was sweating. He was a hard man but Bill was a head case. With that Bill clipped him on the side of the head and Grieve was sliding under the table as Bill slid back the bolt of the door and slipped outside.

There was nothing to be gained from Grieve or any others who had been on the payroll. What he had to do he would do himself. It would lessen the possibility of being shafted.

***

Jamie sat watching TV. He was in a daze. One minute he was happy at what he had done and the next the sheer enormity of what he had done consumed him with abject fear. He had committed murder; well if stabbing a dead man was murder, and now he was unsure of what to do. He had traced his father, wreaked a savage revenge but then failed to achieve anything in his hopelessly unplanned vendetta against Mr. Jacobson. He now realised he should do no more on that score. The risks were too great and what more would he gain. He had rid himself of the shackles of his self-imposed seclusion from the world at large and was in fact now enjoying the freedom he had fought so hard to achieve. 'This should be game over' he thought.

The television droned on. It was literary programme and they were reviewing the latest books. He was about to turn it off when it showed a picture of the cover of a book but he could not see the title but he caught the name of the author as Ruth something. He turned up the volume as the interviewer talked to the author and held up to camera a copy of a weekend magazine with Ruth's picture on the front cover. He was not certain why he was interested except that she was saying how she had decided to write of her experiences after salvaging her life when she had reached rock bottom. There was something familiar about her but he could not pin down what. He sat back as she told the story of her life and remembered he had read the article some weeks before. As she told her story he realised this almost certainly was the same woman he had met those years ago.

He was staggered. Something in him felt pride that despite the sordid nature of their sexual relationship, he had actually done something that had helped someone and she was grateful. At the point where she was saying it would have been nice to thank the man personally he wondered if he should make the effort and contact her. The interview ended with Jamie convinced it was her but doubting whether, in the present circumstances, he should do anything about it.

As the Interviewer was finishing off he said that Ruth was now working with the Police advising on Crime against Children. This brought Jamie to his senses. If she were now connected to the police then the last thing he should be thinking is trying to make contact.

***

Sam dialled the number Ruth had given her. It rang for ages and just as she was about to put the phone down Ruth answered. "Hi Ruth, its Sam. Just seen you on TV. Excellent piece and should help book sales but aren't you a bit concerned at having this out in the open?"

"Hi, thanks Sam. I thought about it but it will help the book and what the hell. I actually owe Jamie my life and whether or not he ever reads it or finds out I'm not ashamed. If it helps someone else so be it."

"Just be careful when you go into the squad room that's all."

Ruth laughed. "OK. When are you coming in for a bite?"

"Not sure. The baby's uncomfortable at the moment and George has a lot on his plate."

"He'll always find time for you."

"I know but I'm doing him a favour by not coming in. Maybe I'll wait till after the baby."

"Sorry Sam, I've got to rush. A meeting has been called on the Balham murder."

"Any developments?"

"Sorry got to go."

The phone went dead and Sam sat at the breakfast bar. It continued to be the most comfortable place.

The phone startled her.

"Hello Ruth, what have you forgotten?"

"Since when has Ruth become a man?" It was the unmistakeable voice of Juan Ramos, although his Spanish accent was much less thick than when she had first met him in Peru.

"You lovely man. When am I going to see you? It's been ages."

"Two weeks since the party, but who's counting? But I want to see you and Eddie to update you on Bill Millichip."

"On the phone?"

"No I'll meet you?"

"Why is something wrong?"

"No I just want to do it in person. I can come to you or meet you somewhere."

"I'll talk to Eddie and get back to you. Would you like to come over for dinner?"

"I'd love to but I'm really up to my neck at the moment. Now I'm not seconded I seem to be needed everywhere at once. I hardly get to go out in the evenings."

"How's Jayne? I really liked her. Bring her over."

"Sorry but Jayne is away on a forensics course. No I want to see you but it will have to be a brief meeting. Can I come over for a coffee when Eddie gets home?"

"OK he'll be in at 5:00 tonight, see you then?"

"I'll be there."

***

Eddie breezed in at 5 on the dot. Sam had not rung him to say Juan was coming but she always knew if he said he would be home at a stated time he would be. She could never work out how he always managed it.

"Hi what's for dinner?"

"Hello yourself. Nothing yet. Juan Ramos is coming to update us about Bill Millichip.

"Why?"

"No idea, just said he wanted to do it personally and not over the phone. Eddie poured himself a Pironi from the fridge. It was a sort of ritual in the summer months and went out to the patio to await Juan. The kids gathered round for cuddles as always and Mark squealed with delight when Sam plonked him on his lap. A car crunched on the gravel driveway and Juan appeared around the side of the house. As always, except on the very hottest of days he was wearing a leather jacket. He must have gone up in the world because this was beautiful lightweight suede that must have cost a fortune.

"Hello Eddie, did Sam tell you I was coming. Nothing sinister but I wanted to talk frankly."

Eddie was amazed at how Juan's English had improved in the years of his secondment from Peru. He even used cockney rhyming slang. "Hi Juan, great to see you again. Where's that gorgeous Jayne?"

"Not you as well." He stopped as Sam came out with a tray of coffees.

"Peruvian blend, we drink nothing else thanks to you. Aren't you the smart one? Going out tonight?"

"Leave him alone Sam. He's probably scared to death of you as it is."

"Not scared Eddie, just in awe. Now let me tell you why I came. Millichip has been in London. He tracked down Grieve who is now out of prison. The meeting obviously did not go well as we found Grieve in a pub near the Elephant and Castle. The landlord called us and Grieve had been pistol whipped on the side of the head and is actually in a coma, so he can't tell us anything. The landlord confirms the description of Bill. He had seen him some years before but the interesting thing is he says he looked ill."

"Good, I hope he's dying."

"Hang on Sam, that's not like you," Eddie said.

"All the trouble he's caused us I don't care."

"He also brought us together."

"So that's a reason to forgive him." Sam's hackles were rising as Juan stepped in.

"We've checked in Argentina and we had not been told the reason he had left the safety of his estancia and travelled to Buenos Aires was he was going to see a cancer specialist. Turns out it might be at an advanced stage but we won't know till we catch him."

"So what does that tell us?"

"Well Sam, what it tells me is he has come home to settle old scores. He's already killed two members of his gang near Manchester and maybe now Grieve. I think, but not everyone agrees, which is why I'm here, he's not got long to live and he wants revenge for Julia's death."

"His own men shot her."

"Yes, but I think he classes Eddie's pursuit of Julia and your surveillance of him as the prime causes of the downfall of his drugs cartel."

"But he wasn't broke. We were told he still had a fortune in Argentina. He could have lived comfortably for the rest of his life."

"Yes Eddie, but Millichip is a vindictive man. I'd bet a lot of money I'm right. He's coming after you."

"So what do we do? You know Sam, she won't hide."

"Dead right I won't."

"Darling, don't say that. What do you suggest?"

"Well we have a surveillance set up to guard you here and I'd prefer Eddie for you to be accompanied on your drive to work. I know you probably think that's over the top but..."

"If you think it's the right thing to do OK."

"Eddie," Sam spluttered "you...."

"Sam, our family safety is the most important thing, nothing else. Our and the kid's safety."

Sam looked thoughtful. "What about the kids?"

"They should be alright if you go along with the surveillance requirements," Juan paused, "but I would prefer them to go with you to stay with your Mother."

"Out of the question," Sam exploded, "I'm not leaving my home because of Bill Millichip."

Eddie and Juan exchanged glances. It would be useless to argue and both knew it.

"Well, that's settled. There's nothing for you to do. I'll give you a list of car numbers and the names of the teams and their mobiles in case you need to speak with them. It won't be covert. It will be upfront and obvious as a deterrent. Lucky you have no close neighbours, wouldn't want to frighten them." Juan smiled and got up to leave. Eddie thanked him for his concern for the family and Sam walked him out to his car.

"Thanks Juan. Sorry I'm tetchy but Millichip always bugs me. Until he's locked away or preferably dead I can't relax. I just know he's coming after us."

"There's nothing I can say to stop you worrying but you know I will do everything to stop him getting to you. Try not to let it get to you. Bye Sam."

She watched Juan as he settled in and fixed his seat belt. She wondered why he was so smartly dressed. He drove out and disappeared scattering the gravel. He seemed in a hurry. Interesting, she thought.

Chapter 19

Sam prepared to see Strachan. Gemma had called the day after Juan's visit. She said it was not important but at the present everything involving the Police gained her utmost attention. The routine of dropping off the kids at mums was a familiar one and as always she nearly missed the train, cutting it too fine. She'd buy the ticket on the train and hope that her lump would get the sympathy of the ticket collector. She would hate to get a fine. Gemma met her as she came out of the lift wearing her visitors' pass.

"Hi Sam. George is in the conference room and would like you to join him."

Sam thought this change of routine was odd, but so much of her life was odd at the moment. They reached the conference room and she was shocked to find it full. It took her aback but George walked to greet her with a hug and a kiss on the cheek. This was designed to relax her and to show how important her presence was in the room. Gemma, asked what she would like to drink but Sam only wanted water.

"Gentlemen, I'm sure Sam needs no introduction within Scotland Yard and I'm pleased she has come." Sam smiled shyly and sat in the seat proffered at the end of the long table next to George. "For your benefit Sam this is free thinking session to discuss all we know about the Millichip case. Your input is welcome."

"Thank you George. Hello everyone. Those who know me will understand once a copper always a copper. I still think about the job every day. Even with this lump." She could see a few smiles and she started to relax. Juan Ramos was not present and she wondered why. George may have sensed this. "Juan is on his way."

George asked each of the eleven men in the room to update him on aspects of the case. Most significant were the contributions of Billy Day and Andy Pride who had gone to Argentina to bring Millichip back on the extradition warrant. Much of what was said seemed old news but Sam knew it was crucial to keep going over everything time and time again so anything that might have been overlooked or down played could become significant. It was new to hear of the violence of the deaths of Garry and John Briggs in Manchester. Sam shuddered at the description of carnage when the police eventually found the car at the farm. She realised how lucky she was to have escaped from the camp in the mountains near Machu Picchu.

Of great interest was the artist's impression of what Bill might look like now. Whilst it was only a few years ago his appearance had been changed on the assumption he might be in the final stages of cancer.

"Juan told me his opinion was he was coming to settle old scores before he died. Clearly he hasn't lost his strength. He killed the Briggs brothers and Grieve, so he's still a major threat."

"Make no mistake, he is still a threat." Sam turned in her seat to see Juan who had just walked through the door. "Sorry I'm late but I have some news." A seat was placed for Juan and it was obvious his colleagues had a great deal of respect for him.

"What's new then Juan?" George always showed him respect; always calling him by his first name, not usual in the hierarchical police force.

"I have just heard from my sources in Peru that officers in Argentina have visited Millichip's estancia and interviewed the farm manager and the old man who runs the house. The farm manager and gauchos know very little. The old man, his name is Angelo is in his eighties and has been with the family since he was a boy. He is like a father to Bill Millichip and was very distraught when he found out Bill was ill. Now he knows Bill has left the country and probably won't return and he will eventually have the job of transferring ownership to the families who have worked there all their lives. This is in accordance with Millichip's wishes."

"This makes it clear he is here to settle scores. So the surveillance on Sam and Eddie will be crucial. You called it right, what else Juan?"

"He has been seen in London and attacked Grieve. It is amazing he seems to have no loyalty from the underworld and we may get lucky someone shops him."

"What else?"

"Not much, well nothing really. We have the teams sorted out. They have copies of old pictures and what he might look like. I have designated John Cooper to be Eddie's driver although Eddie insists on driving. He's going on a kidnap evasion course."

This was news to Sam but she resisted making a comment. She was secretly pleased that Eddie was getting on with things without worrying her. Maybe with the baby so imminent she should relax more than she could with this hanging over her. She was running over the whole scenario in her mind and not paying attention to the further discussion around the table when she became aware Ruth had entered the room. Some got up to leave and a couple of new faces arrived.

"Sam that's all on Millichip and I now need to spend a few minutes on the Balham murder. Your welcome to stay and then we'll have a bite to eat."

"Thanks George, I'll stay if you don't mind."

Ruth and a new team started on an update of the Michaels murder but Sam was letting it pass over her head. She was dying to know from Ruth whether there had been any reaction to her TV interview. She wished she had excused herself as she became increasingly uncomfortable with the leather chairs. Fortunately the meeting was interrupted when Gemma called in to say George was required for a meeting upstairs. Everybody got up as George helped Sam to her feet and Ruth would take her to lunch. This was particularly pleasing to Sam. She was dying to find out more of Ruth's weird story.

***

Jamie had come to a conclusion. Not much had happened that was good in his life but Ruth had been good. He had to try to make contact. Something was compelling him to do so despite the dangers; she was working with the police and he had just killed his father. He pondered how best to make contact; first of all he would Google her name and then view the web coverage of the news interview.

He was able to obtain a contact e-mail address but that would mean he would have to contact her from his computer. He was definitely keen to make contact initially by phone; it would be safer.

The web coverage allowed him the option of contacting the TV station to see if he could get in touch that way. The web was as always the provider; it gave details of Ruth's publisher and editorial links to the BBC who had produced the documentary. As so often in his recent searches he seemed to hit lucky. He telephoned the publisher and got through to the Production Office.

"Hello, I'm trying to get in contact with Ruth Danson–Whyte and I wondered if you had a phone number for her?"

"I'm sorry but we aren't allowed to give out contact information on our clients. I'm sure you appreciate…"

Jamie cut in "I certainly appreciate that but I am the man referred to in the story she has written."

This had an immediate effect. "Excuse me but how can I be sure that you are that person?"

"Well if I could speak to Ruth I'm sure she could identify me."

"Hold the line for a moment."

Jamie could sense a cupped hand over the mouthpiece at the other end and after a minute the phoned clicked and a new voice came on.

"Hello, my name is Ed and I'm the controller here. Could you give me your address and a contact phone and I'll check whether Ruth wishes to speak with you."

"It says on in the article she does so what's the problem."

"No problem, but we have to be careful in such matters. Give me your name, address and a phone number and I will pass it on to her."

Jamie refused the demand for an address and said he would only provide a mobile number. The man reluctantly agreed. This was a 'pay as you go' phone so provided no link to his home although he assumed if the police wished to trace the call they could get his location. So he decided when he was at home he would leave it switched off and the call would divert to his messaging service.

Jamie sat back looking out of the window at the street below. It was a bright sunny day. So much had happened to him in the five months since he had been attacked; some of it not so good but in the main he felt liberated. He could walk the streets, felt comfortable enough for confrontation with his past although the encounter with Jacobson had been a disaster. Now he hoped he might meet the woman who had been such a brief but comforting part of his past before he had subsided into his long and seemingly reclusive spell.

It was two days later when he was out the phone rang. It was a message to ring his service. The caller was a woman asking him to ring another mobile phone number. Whether this was Ruth he had no idea but he was excited at the prospect. He punched the number but his hands were shaking and he twice misdialled. Then he was through. The ringing seemed to get louder and louder as if beckoning him.

A hesitant voice answered. "Who is it?"

"My name is Jamie and I'm trying to contact Ruth."

"That's me."

"I read your article and saw the TV interview. I think I'm the one you referred to. Could we meet?"

"Well, I'm not sure that would be a good idea, certainly not alone."

"We could meet in a public place, a café perhaps. I don't mind if you bring a friend. It really is your call; you said you might have liked to thank the person so here's your chance."

"You know I work with the police would you mind if I bring a colleague?"

Jamie started to get worried. Maybe this was not a good idea. His mind was racing.

"Are you still there?" Ruth had sensed a difficulty and was keen to go through with meet. It had great possibilities for publicity for the book launch. "What if I bring a girlfriend, she's not a policewoman and she's heavily pregnant. Would that be better?"

Jamie wondered whether to go through with this. It could be a big mistake. What if he were featured in an article, might Jacobson see the picture and it rekindle their confrontation? He might then decide to do something about their encounter. He wanted to see Ruth, he had no real idea why but he was curious and it was one of the better episodes in his miserable existence. "Yes that would be OK with me."

"Do you come into London often?"

"Virtually never but I will. Where do you want to meet and when?"

"I'll need to set it up with my friend first and then choose a place. She only comes in once a fortnight so I'll ring you in a few days to let you know. Are there any days that are bad for you?"

Jamie smiled at the thought of his non-existent diary. "No most days are free."

"Then I'll get back to you shortly. Thank you for contacting me."

Jamie switched off the phone. He was strangely exhilarated as he walked back to his flat but what had he done? Had he made a trap to fall into? After years of anonymity now he might be in the spotlight. How stupid a decision was that? He had time to think about it and he need not carry it through.

***

Sam was dozing in her favourite armchair. She was comfortable for the first time in weeks of sitting only at the breakfast bar. The harsh ringing of the phone startled her. 'Who could that be?' she wondered. Might it be the police with news about the surveillance? It was Ruth.

"Hello Sam, I hope I'm not disturbing you?"

"No," Sam lied, "I was just sitting having a cup of tea. How nice to hear from you. Nothing wrong I hope?"

"No, I have some news for you. You remember my telling you of the young man who befriended me when I was at rock bottom?"

"Who, James was it?"

"Jamie. He's made contact. Said he saw the interview and read the supplement. Want's to meet."

"What? You mean he's made contact with you? That's a bit weird isn't it?"

"I suppose so, hadn't quite thought of it that way. Anyway I wanted to find him and he's found me. Want's to meet but I said not alone. Would you come with me? I know it's a liberty asking and you in your condition."

Sam didn't know whether to be reticent or pleased she had been asked but jumped at the chance. "Yes of course. Sounds exciting but you need to be careful. He might be a mad axe man for all you know." Sam laughed at the absurdity of what she had just said.

"We'll go armed," she paused, "with heavy handbags."

"When and where?"

"I've still to ring him back. Didn't want to until I'd sounded you out."

"My diary is free except an antenatal clinic next Wednesday."

"Ok thanks Sam, I'll get back to you. It will be a coffee shop somewhere near the office. I won't tell him but I may tape the conversation."

"Isn't that a bit dishonest?"

"Precautionary in case anything goes wrong. I'll speak soon. Bye Sam."

***

Jamie travelled up to Central London for the first time since he had gone through to Hatfield towards the end of May to confront Jacobson. He just wanted to walk around so that he felt more comfortable when he met Ruth. He was not going anywhere near his father's shop but he was interested to know what had happened to it since his death. It was another 3 days before Ruth contacted him to fix the meeting in a coffee shop in the Broadway near St James Park underground station. He had looked at the map and seen that was very near New Scotland Yard but he decided there was nothing sinister; it was just near her work. The meeting was set for Tuesday of the next week. It seemed an age away but he had waited all this time so what was another few days.

***

George Strachan was sitting in his office having a quiet moment running through the Michaels murder. They had made little progress since spotting the same person following Michaels out of the underground on consecutive nights. There had been insufficient resolution to identify the man. No further leads had come up from the sandwich shop and the café opposite. He was catching flack from upstairs despite having caught the Tooting murderer almost by chance after two months. It had been down to DS Dick Williamson and his dogged pursuance of procedure that a routine 'stop and search' had led to further investigation and the killer had been identified. The luck was that so many routine 'stop and searches' take place the files rarely get checked a second time. Dick had been thorough and placed the lad in Tooting within half an hour of the killing. Good solid police work would see Dick being promoted to Detective Inspector at some stage soon but he'd only just transferred in so it might have to wait.

He had not noticed Ruth standing at the door. "A word please, if you have a moment?"

"Come in and have a seat." George somehow had more time for Ruth since he knew how well she and Sam got on. "What's up?"

"Just letting you know in case you think it's a bad idea."

"Sounds ominous."

"You know about my past. The whole world knows. Jamie, the man in the story has made contact. Says he saw the interview and wanted to get in touch."

"And you're worried?"

"Sam sowed the seeds of doubt. I asked if she would come along. I told him I would not see him alone and he said he'd prefer it not to be a police colleague."

"Sensible woman, that Sam. Instinct says don't go but womanly curiosity will override that. Sam would be a good choice but for her current condition. If there is a risk she's normally the right person but I'd hate her to be involved if things were to turn nasty."

"That's really unlikely in a crowded coffee shop."

"I would remind you a great many crimes are committed in public places."

"But why would he want to hurt me?"

"You tell me. What I suggest so it can take place in safety is that we have a plain clothes policewoman in the coffee shop keeping an eye on you both."

"Fine with me. Thanks."

"Give Gemma the details. Thanks for telling me."

Ruth left his office smiling to fix up the meeting with Jamie and Sam. She had got exactly what she wanted and hadn't even had to ask.

George resumed his cogitation of the Balham murder and was no further into solving the case. The footprint cast had not led anywhere and what DNA evidence there was at the scene showed no match to any known criminals for whom they had DNA samples. He needed a breakthrough or he might find new blood being brought into the investigation.

Chapter 20

Bill Millichip was having a bad day. He had been sick in the night. It was the first time he had really felt this awful. He needed treatment but that was out of the question. He was now a 'stateless' person. His passport was Spanish but the only part of the world he really knew was South America and now Argentina was out of the question. There were still Central American states where he could get lost but cash was now the problem. He prided himself on having money stashed in various countries but some of his numerous credit card accounts had been frozen. For accounts in a number of different names now to be unavailable he realised the net was closing in on him. His problem was he had about £1,000 with him including the money he had taken from Garry at the farmhouse. It was increasingly looking as though he would have to commit further crime to get cash but he was no armed robber and he was alone.

This crusade to avenge Julia's death now seemed a poor idea. He looked at his contacts list on his mobile. He would keep ringing old contacts to see if anything turned up. He was now using a 'pay as you go' phone so his calls could not be traced. Somehow he needed to find one person who would still repay the favours owed. He had rung six out of the seven men who had been part of the old firm. Six wasted calls; they were either in prison or slammed down the phone on him. The seventh call brought a ray of hope. It was the girlfriend of one of his gang who picked up the phone.

"Hello," the voice was tentative as though calls never came through to the phone, "who is it?"

"Is Geoff there?"

"No, who wants him?"

"Bill Millichip."

"Well I never. You've a nerve. Geoff's banged up in Wormwood Scrubs at present. Something to do with you wasn't it?"

Bill thought for a moment. He was pretty sure her name was Elaine. He could act tough, but where would that get him, or be contrite.

"Elaine I'm sorry to hear that. It seems we all suffered."

"You, suffered. Not bloody likely. Pissed off to South America and living it up while the foot soldiers got shafted. Anyway it's nice you remember me."

"Not shafted by me. They all knew the risks. All lived well but it came to an end, as it has for me. I've come back for a final goodbye. I have a package for Geoff."

"What's in it?"

He wondered what might get him further in this conversation. She was his last link with the past and perhaps, just an outside chance, she might be useful. "It's a long story but I have some cash that Geoff was due. I'm actually dying of cancer and I want him to benefit. Sort of conscience money if you like."

"Oh God, I'm sorry. Do you want to come round, or shall I come to you?"

Bill smiled to himself. "OK, I'll come, still the same place?"

"Yes, when can you come?"

"Straight away if that's OK?"

"Half past six. Do you want a bite to eat?"

Bill remembered Elaine; classier than the average, it might be interesting. Other than that, female company might perk him up. "Great, half past six it is."

***

Bill got ready. He dressed to impress. No point in disappointing the lady. His hotel was very jaded and luxuriating in the bath with stained tiles did not do much to brighten his spirits but the thought of Elaine had started to excite him. He arrived at the house having paid off the taxi two streets away and carefully approached the house. He had been once before when he delivered Geoff home after a particularly big binge. From memory they were flush with cash and had blown a couple of grand on women and booze that night.

It was a modern detached house, not large but well maintained with a neat garden. He wondered who kept it that way, not Elaine's scene he thought. He rang the bell and could hear Elaine from the top of the stairs shouting to come in. He pushed the door, it was unlocked. Clearly Elaine had more taste than Geoff and business had not been entirely bad.

She came down the stairs preceded by waves of Chanel No 5. Not an unpleasant smell by any means but a trifle overpowering. She had taken a lot of trouble. She looked stunning. She must have been 40 but she looked 25. She wasn't a natural blond but it suited her and the short hair added a touch of class. Her dress showed of her breasts and cleavage as she arrived at the foot of the stairs she held out her hand and Bill rather self-consciously shook it. She smiled and led him to the lounge.

"What are you drinking?"

"Scotch and water, no ice, if you have it?"

"Sit down, back in a moment."

Bill was confused. He was here to see if he could somehow get money to continue his crusade or at worst escape from the UK. Elaine gave him his drink; a large one and she had a glass of white wine. She explained Geoff was eligible for parole in 18 months. He had been sent down for GBH whilst resisting arrest when the net closed in.

"Geoff was stupid," Elaine seemed anxious to set the record straight, "he knew he was going to be arrested and with you gone he could have had it easy as a foot soldier but he got cocky and when the police started getting tough he cocked up and look what it got him; nearly twice the sentence."

Bill was surprised at her frankness but decided to play along until a plan of action became clear. "We all know it can't last. We all get it in the end. Still I'm sorry the way it worked out for him and for you."

"Don't worry about me. When he gets out I'm not sure what I'm going to do. I like my life at the moment. Play golf and socialise. Go out with men but won't let myself get trapped into something permanent. There's none of the old lot around so he's not going to know is he?"

"I lied when I said I had a package for him." Bill had no idea why he said it; somehow his life had always been a lie; cheating came easily to him. "Truth is I'm in a hole and need help myself."

"You in a hole?"

"Yeah. Down to my last thousand and no credit, likely to be dead I don't know when and lost for what to do next." He actually meant what he said but felt he must be getting soft in the head.

"I knew you weren't coming to give Geoff a package."

"Then why invite me?"

"Curiosity. Wanted to know what you looked like now. We are quite comfortable thanks to the old firm. Anyway you never know what the evening might bring? Let's eat and reminisce about the old days."

The meal was excellent and the large scotch and a couple of glasses of wine had mellowed Bill. His recent melancholy seemed to have melted away and he was 'out on a date.' He was comfortable in the knowledge that Elaine must have envisaged something might happen so why disappoint her. He was about to start his favourite chat line when she leant across the table and squeezed his hand.

"How long since you last had it?"

"Truth? Six months and then it was the housekeeper's daughter. Not very romantic."

"Let's see what we can do about that," and she pushed her chair back making a scraping noise on the wood block floor, "that's if you're up to it."

"Never failed before." He allowed her to lead him to the stairs and he followed her watching the seductive sway of the hips. Her bedroom was definitely a ladies boudoir. He could not see Geoff being comfortable in it. Maybe she had other plans for him.

She turned to face him and they kissed. He was tentative, uncertain but she was wanting more. Her tongue darted and Bill knew he should let her lead. This had never been his custom but somehow on this night in this place it was the right thing to do. He held her and kissed her more passionately and she responded. She rubbed her thigh against his crotch. His erection was growing, her hand slid down and massaged him. He slipped one strap of her dress off her shoulder, then the other. The zip at the back seemed stuck but she turned and he could see there was a clasp. As he unzipped her dress he felt heady with excitement. The dress fell to the floor exposing a black lacy bra and tiny panties. Before he could undo her she turned and started to unbutton his shirt. He was nervous but she seemed in total control. She struggled with his belt and then undid his trousers. He felt foolish as they slid to the floor around his ankles. His erection was now complete and she pulled his boxer shorts down.

"Lay with me for a while, Bill. Let's not hurry."

Bill undid her bra exposing her breasts. She was not large, her breasts were not page three, far from it, they were on the small side, but perfectly formed with large nipples. He cupped her left breast in his hand and fondled her nipple. It was hard. He knew she wanted him and to put it mildly he was desperate for her. He hooked a finger into her pants and started to pull them down. She helped and kicked them off and pulled him towards the large king size. He lay on his back as she took off his socks and now both naked they lay holding each other.

"Bill can I ask you something?"

"Depends."

"Geoff said you fancied that policewoman, what was her name?"

"Sam. What of it?"

"Did you have her?"

Bill sensed no point in lying anymore, his pride was already hurt. "No, I tried but she kneed me in the balls. But I did fancy her. She had a body to die for; like yours."

"My tits are too small and my arse is getting too big."

"Not just because we're in bed together but for the record you are a cracking bird, tits just perfect and an arse, well that's built to provide thrust."

She giggled. "How long do you have?"

"All night."

"No, the cancer?"

"No idea, had no formal diagnosis yet. Was on my way to hospital when the police got me."

"How did you get away?"

"Plenty of friends in Buenos Aeries. But no more. So I could have years. It could be treatable but how am I going to find out, or I could be dead in weeks. Somehow there's not much point in worrying. Enough chat I need you, I want you Elaine."

They made love immediately. She came on top of him but he came before she reached orgasm. They lay quietly together. It seemed an embarrassing silence to Bill and he dropped off to sleep. It was dark and he could feel Elaine stirring. He turned to see her sitting on the edge of the bed. Was she crying?

"What's the matter?"

"Nothing. Certainly not worrying about Geoff but I really thought it was going to be great tonight. I like you."

"Tonight's not finished, is it? Come here."

She got back under the duvet and snuggled up to him. Bill's body showed no sign of the cancer he thought he had, his six-foot frame was still well muscled and he had not lost all of his good looks. He'd never had trouble with women, except Sam that is. He kissed her gently and as she responded he climbed on her. He was ready and she guided him into her and gasped as he thrust into her. They made love and this time he was in control. He brought her to orgasm quickly then slowly ground into her until she came again and he exploded in her. This was beautiful sex. Nothing sordid. Sex between a lonely man and a woman, confident and in her prime.

They lay panting and she held him tight. "You were delicious. That is the best sex I've ever had. Where have you been all my life?"

All Bill could say was "Thanks."

She laughed and that made it better. They were lovers, if only for this one night.

Bill was awoken by sounds downstairs. Elaine was in the kitchen and he could smell coffee and toast. He found a bathrobe hanging on the door and slipped it on. It was little on the tight size but it was for a man. He padded downstairs.

"Hi. Didn't mean to wake you. Here's coffee."

"Thanks, I haven't slept as well for ages."

"Me neither. We should do it again sometime."

"Best offer I've had. Seriously you should not get hooked up with me. The police are looking for me and one way or another I'm going to be dead. Either natural causes or shot evading capture. There's no way I'm doing bird."

"Stay for today. I've not felt this horny for some time. We owe it to ourselves."

"What about Geoff?"

"What about him? What he doesn't know won't hurt him. Anyway I have plans before he gets out."

"What sort of plans?"

"Put it this way they don't involve him."

"Bit harsh?"

"He has it coming. He's no saint. I know what he's been up to with other women. There's not a lot a woman can't find out from washing a man's clothes."

Bill was about to speak but she put her hand over his mouth.

"Not your business. Just enjoy the moment. I have and no regrets, not one bit."

"You're quite some woman Elaine, why I never saw it before I do not know."

"Make the most of it now then."

"Give me a break. After breakfast."

Elaine laughed and busied herself making scrambled eggs. "This OK? I've got no bacon. Don't generally have men staying overnight. Then we need to see if there is anything I can do to help you out."

Bill was happy to be cosseted and left it there. He needed to make decisions and he was now unwilling to involve Elaine or to hurt her. His original plan was to see if she had money and if necessary to use violence to get it.

***

Sam met Ruth at the stairs at the top of St James's Park station. Although now more than comfortably off she never used taxis despite her condition. She thought it kept her grounded.

"Hi Sam. It's exciting don't you think. After all these years wondering, I'm now going to be reacquainted with Jamie."

"Don't get too excited. He may not show. It might be the biggest disaster…"

"Sam, this is in the realms of research. It's past, nothing can come of it and I would not want it to. It's closure, that's all. Anyway let me tell you George insisted that a plainclothes police woman is going to be in the café just in case."

"In case what?"

"In case nothing. It's just because you are here. He's very protective, especially where you are concerned."

They reached the coffee shop, which was almost empty. Of the ten tables only three were occupied. Sam could spot the policewoman. Years of training allowed her to pick out the unusual. There was not the slightest hint of recognition. They sat in the window seat and ordered café latte for Ruth and bottled water for Sam and waited. They were five minutes early but after fifteen nobody who could have been Jamie appeared. Then as they were beginning to think it was all a waste of time a man walked in. To say he was short was an understatement. He was wearing a smart lightweight bomber jacket with blue chinos and white shirt. It was his shoes that let him down, scuffed, not polished.

"I'm Jamie," he said shyly exposing immaculate teeth that seemed not to match the rest of his face. He was not handsome, far from it but Sam thought there was something endearing about him, "I'm sorry I'm late. I nearly didn't come at all."

"Hello Jamie. This is my friend Sam. I said I would bring someone. We've not known each other long but we're good friends. I'm glad you did come. Would you like a drink?"

"Coffee, please. But I'll get it."

The lady on the counter said she would bring it across and Jamie sat down.

"I'm not sure why I got in contact. My life's been a mess, been a bit of a recluse for years. Bullied at school and bullied in life but recently I've got hold of myself and get out more. I got beaten up in the street and it made me determined to get hold of my life. Bit like you Ruth. The bottom's not very nice is it? Sorry I'm rambling on."

"I'm pleased you rang. You can't know how important you are in my life without knowing it. But for you I'd probably be dead and now I'm happy and successful. You've presumably read what happened after our little liaison," she smiled at him, "going to see the Nuns and getting sorted but what about you?"

"My mum had died when I was taking exams. She died of cancer and hadn't told me until the last few months. I never knew my father, he buggered off before I was born. My mum left me a lot of money, all in cash. She told me she'd had to keep us by selling herself, sort of call girl, not a street prostitute. I idolised her, it made no difference to me what she did. Anyway I failed my exams because my teacher did nothing to help me. He was a sadistic bastard. Sorry for my language."

"No problem."

"I left school and had various jobs until one boss was particularly vicious bully and I'd had enough so for the past year I stayed at home living frugally off mum's money."

Sam thought about intervening. She was sure she knew Jamie from her past but this was Ruth's day. Ruth and Jamie chatted and Sam almost felt like a voyeur when they talked openly about the occasions they had spent together. The conversation appeared to have exhausted itself. There were longer pregnant pauses so Sam decided to ask.

"Jamie, I hope you don't mind me asking but what school did you go to?"

"It was called St Francis…"

"I thought so Jamie. So it is you. I went there too. You were in the same year as me. There was something familiar about you."

"What, five foot and a bit?" he smiled.

"Well I never, what a small world. I never knew why you suddenly left. You were top of your class and the word was you would go to Uni after 'A' levels."

"Long story, partly mum's death but I know it was much more about Jacobson. He was my form teacher and he was just one of the people who bullied me." Jamie suddenly thought he should not say too much. There still had to be a possibility that Jacobson might have filed a report of their encounter with the police. "That's life – just got to get on with it." He said trying to make light of it.

Sam's intervention appeared to have made Jamie nervous and he seemed anxious to end the meeting. "I'd better be going. I'm glad I came, Ruth. Our meetings meant a lot, never forgotten but time has moved on. Thanks for the coffee. Nice meeting you Sam."

With that, he slipped on his jacket and walked out and was gone. The policewoman also took the opportunity to leave, giving Sam and Ruth a knowing look.

"Well, who's more surprised Sam, you or me?"

***

Elaine looked at Bill. There was something about him that made her want to look after him. It wasn't just he was a good catch, if she'd found him before Geoff she might have wanted to be with him. It wasn't that Geoff wasn't good looking but he looked cheap. He had villain stamped all over him whereas Bill looked for all the world like a businessman. She was still tingling with excitement at the thought he had agreed to stay. Another session in bed was a mouth-watering prospect, but she needed to know what he wanted.

"Are the police chasing you now for the old crime or something new?"

"What's it matter?"

"Only that old crimes, they aren't so proactive."

"How do you know?"

"I don't."

"I got into some bother up in Manchester after I arrived. Two guys ended up dead. They left me no choice so I assume that hots things up if they believe it's me, but there's nothing to tie me into it?"

"Were they strangers or did you know them?"

"They worked for me."

"You killed your own men?"

"Look Elaine, it's none of your business and you're better not knowing."

"Doesn't make me feel any better though. If you can do it to your own maybe you could kill me?"

"Give it a rest. Why would I kill a beautiful woman who has done me no harm?"

"Let's change the subject shall we? Will you have dinner with me tonight?"

"And afters?"

"Definitely afters. I need to go to Tesco to get some milk. Would you like a steak?"

"Great."

"Do you want to come with me? You can sit in the car if you don't want to go in."

"No thanks. I'll sit here and regain my strength."

"Help yourself to anything, coffee, tea or drinks."

Bill watched her leave and then set about searching the house for money. Villains always kept large amounts of cash, safer than banks and the taxman never knows. He was careful to search without leaving evidence and at last he found a tin box with old papers but underneath was wad of £50 notes. He was guessing there must be about £1,000. He paused wondering whether to take the money and leave. He didn't want to do that to Elaine but she might not know the money was there. The alternative was to ask her for help and see what happened. If he had to he would take it but that might mean getting tough with her. She didn't deserve that. She was good woman and he genuinely liked her. Anyway he fancied sex and a steak so the decision could wait.

***

Elaine puzzled as she drove to Tesco. The death of her best friend's husband had been a shock. But if you live by the sword you die by the sword and Garry had been one mean hard bastard. She had known Garry from the age of 15 and she had never met a more devoted couple. What was she to do? She was now having sex with the man who had killed Garry and his brother. One thing was certain she'd have to be very careful.

She could turn him in; there was probably a reward. If she rang the police it could all be over before she had to return. "What to do next is a real conundrum?" she said to the car mirror.

The fact that she arrived home with steaks and red wine indicated to her there might be a variety of outcomes. One for certain was she wanted to have sex with him at least once more.

"Fix me a gin and tonic." She shouted up the stairs but there was no reply. "Bill." She walked up the stairs slowly calling his name but he wasn't there. "Bill, where are you?" Then it struck her and she went straight to her tin box but there it was in her hiding place as she left it. She started back downstairs but decided to look in the box and it dawned on her he had come looking for money and had used her. "Bastard." She screamed then started crying.

She went back to the kitchen and there on the worktop was note. With trembling hands she read it:

> 'Elaine,
>
> Don't think too harshly but I'm desperate. I have things to do, scores to settle before I die. I needed money and I didn't have the guts to ask in case you said no.
>
> Last night was the most beautiful night I have ever spent. You are such a lovely person and to be involved with me could only cause you greater hurt in the long run.
>
> If I ever get the chance I will send you the money plus some.
>
> Bill'

Elaine's eyes filled with tears. Such a lovely note but such a cowardly way to leave. She'd have probably given him some money but not all of it.

She picked up the phone and dialled Wormwood Scrubs. She asked for a call to Geoff. She would tell him Bill had come and robbed her but leave out everything else. What he did with the information was up to him. She would not ring the police; it was not the way people like her did things.

A time was agreed for the phone call to Geoff and she told him about Bill stealing the money.

"Jesus 'Laine. Why did you let him in the house? You must have guessed he wanted something." Elaine half smiled at the comment. Geoff's outrage knew no bounds and he decided Bill would pay dearly. "I'll make some calls, someone will track him down and when they do he's dead meat."

"You may have to work fast. First he's dying of cancer and second he's going to get revenge for his sister. He knows he's dead one way or the other. If they want him they only have to stay that copper Sam and her husband."

"You seem to have found out a lot for a chance meeting."

"Well you know what a charmer Bill is, he couldn't stop bragging about what he wanted to do."

"We'll talk about it another time. Gotta go. Bye Love and thanks for ringing."

***

Bill had returned to his hotel and grabbed a small bag. He need to be on the move but couldn't carry all he had brought with him. His clothes were still in the room so he walked out without paying his bill. To pay with cash would use up what he had and use of a card wouldn't have worked but would alert the authorities. He was uncertain of what to do next but he went to an internet café to research what he could about Sam. He was surprised how much coverage there was about her and the gallantry award she had received. The story in one newspaper referred to her wedding to Eddie and his return to the consultancy he had so suddenly abandoned in his search for Julia; that ill-fated search that had brought about the death of his sister and now the end of his life in Argentina. The two of them would have to pay for all that carnage.

There was even an interview with Vince at his Abbey Road offices. This was where Bill would start. He had not shaved since he had stayed with Elaine so the emerging beard would help to disguise him, should Eddie have even got a glimpse of him before he was shot. He must have been shown police photos but that was a few years ago and even some of his friends, if he had any left, might not recognise him in the street. He set out for Abbey Road from St John's Wood Underground station. The offices, just as in the photograph when the interview was covered in the newspapers, were right in front of him.

He walked past on the opposite side of the road and then back again. Ideally he would need to stake out the place. He could steal a car, no problem but it was a main road and he could not park unless he could gain access to the private parking of the apartments opposite. He decided that was his best approach and returned at about 4.30 pm in the hope of seeing him and following him to see where he lived.

He found a car parked illegally on a side street. It took him no time to open the door. The car was a late model Astra, black with alloy wheels and it was a rental. The papers showed it was rented to an American couple from Iowa and they had left the spare key in the glove box. They had also left some food, which presumably they planned for their picnic. Bill drove to an old red brick Victorian apartment block and sat in a space in the private car park diagonally opposite the offices. The office started to empty around 5 o'clock but no sign of Eddie until at a quarter to six he came out. It was definitely him and Bill was surprised at how fit and well he looked. Bill started the motor and backed out and into the exit so he could follow Eddie's Porsche as it slid into Abbey Road heading north. Bill followed at a discreet distance but was keen not to let too many cars between him and Eddie. Eddie was driving expertly through the traffic and Bill had to take risks and twice jumped a red light. He followed him out past Elstree and turned into a leafy lane in a well-heeled area with beautiful houses. It was then Bill saw the police car parked near the driveway that Eddie entered. Bill carried on without looking. So he now knew where they lived but also they were having permanent police protection, except he was certain no other car had followed Eddie.

***

Eddie walked through the front door to be greeted by the usual screaming of the girls as they ran to him. Sam was looking as though she would be giving birth very soon, she looked tired and huge.

"You OK? You're looking tired. Are you doing too much?"

"Hello to you to. I'm fine. Did you drive alone? Where was your escort?"

"He wasn't well so I told him to go home."

"But you were the one wanting us to be careful."

"I know, but it turned out OK."

"Men!" Sam turned and went to the kitchen. Eddie dropped his jacket on a chair and followed her. He grabbed her and kissed her neck. "Umm. I like it when you do that… but that's as far as you're going to get. The kids need bathing."

That night Eddie slept fitfully. He was actually annoyed he had put himself at risk on the drive home. As he dressed for business he wondered whether to ask for one of the two policemen outside to accompany him but Sam's safety was his main concern. He hopped into the car and nodded to the police car as he turned onto the lane. If they were surprised he was on his own they didn't show it. After about a mile at a sharp corner a black Astra came out of a farm gate and forced him to swerve onto the bank. Eddies instincts were quick and he avoided a crash and still stayed on the road. He was about to get out of the car when he heard a loud crack and the side window of his Porsche shattered. He could not see the driver of the Astra but quickly accelerated away and rang the emergency number he had been given. They were quick to answer.

"Hi Eddie Jacobs. I'm on Langley Lane and I've been attacked but I've got away driving to the A1."

"Who was it?"

"Black Astra but couldn't see the driver. No idea of the plates."

"Keep driving on the A1 but go north as there's no traffic and we'll intercept you at the Hatfield Galleria cut and cover. Got it? Stop for no one unless it's a marked police car and don't worry about speeding. We'll alert Sam's crew."

Eddie was tempted to turn around but that would have been crazy. He dialled Sam and was relieved when she answered. "Listen and don't argue. Lock the doors and close the windows and don't open unless you recognise them. Bill's been around, he tried to force me off the road and shot at me."

"Eddie, are you hurt?"

"No. The police know and by now they will be getting to the house. I'll come home when I've met them. I've had to go to Hatfield then I'll be straight back."

"Why Hatfield?"

"I'll explain everything when I get there. Do as I say and lock up and stay upstairs and away from the windows."

Eddie could hear a police siren and looked in his mirror but there was no car.

"The police have arrived. There must a couple of cars coming up the drive."

"OK I'll see you shortly." Eddie rang off and approached the slip road before the Hatfield cut and cover. There was a police car with flashing blue lights on the bridge and it tucked in behind and indicated him to stop. He sat there and for the first time realised his heart was pounding. He opened the door and the policeman smiled.

"Not often you get told to drive fast is it Sir? You okay? When you're ready we'll escort you back home. Your family is fine. Mind if I hop in with you. Best in the circumstances."

"No, I don't mind. I feel stupid as my regular guard felt unwell yesterday and I told him to go home. Got a bollocking from my wife."

"Probably get another from us."

They set off for home with the early morning cool air blowing through the shattered window. He arrived to find Sam making tea for the assembled army. She broke off and ran to him and held him tight. "I'll speak to you later." She whispered threateningly in his ear.

The phone rang. It was George Strachan wanting a full update. "Sam I want you to move out for a while. He knows where you live. There are plenty of places in those leafy lanes he could hide. Juan is on his way. I must insist you do what he says. Put Eddie on."

Sam decided resistance was not sensible. "George wants a word." Eddie took the phone and wandered off to the sitting room. His conversation with George was short. George was not up for discussion.

"We're all off to your mum's. Grab some things. Once we've seen Juan we'll be going."

Sam was relieved the decision had been taken out of her hands. She had been determined not to be a prisoner in her own home but that is precisely what she would be. If anything happened to Eddie and the kids, she could not live with herself.

That night she fell into a deep sleep. She dreamt strange things. She woke up at one point in a sweat and was relieved to see Eddie sleeping peacefully alongside her. She could not get back to sleep for quite some time but when she did she relived that day on the mountain in Peru. It was as vivid as the day it had happened. First, the moment when Eddie had blundered into the camp and the screaming and shouting, then the retort of the gun. She was only yards away and then she saw Eddie fall to the ground.

She had no idea how long it was before she took off down the path she had previously chosen as one of her planned escape routes, but it must have been instinctive. Her heart had been thumping as she hid in the bushes and heard the man charging down the path.

She instinctively knew as he stopped she would be caught. She remembered the awful smell of him as he grappled her to the ground and put all his weight on her, he had tried to kiss her, she could feel his rough hands as he grabbed her breasts then ran his hand to her belt. She thought she was going to die but not before something even worse. It was when he lifted his body to pull her jeans down that she had kneed him in the groin and in the struggle a shot rang out. She could feel the heat and cordite was almost choking her. She had grabbed the gun in his hand and twisting it away from her and it had gone off. He had rolled off clutching his chest and was dead within seconds.

She awoke with a start and looked over at Eddie who was still sleeping peacefully. She was caked in sweat and went to the bathroom to wash herself. She could not sleep for the rest of the night but vowed to tell Eddie everything that had happened that day in the jungle.

***

Bill had been lucky. He drove after Eddie but had lost him. He knew the alert would have gone out so he crossed over the roundabout with the A1 and headed to Aldenham and Stanmore where he dumped the car in a car park and walked to Stanmore station for the Jubilee line to the West End. What next, he wondered? Eddie would have much closer protection; it would be much more difficult to get close.

George Strachan stormed into the squad room. "Who in God's name let Eddie Jacobs drive from his office alone?"

"Smith was unwell and Mr Jacobs sent him home Guvnor. Nobody knew until after the shooting."

"Where's Smith now?"

"He's still off sick."

"He won't feel too good when he gets back either. All details are to be doubled up. The family is moving to Stanmore where her mother lives. There will be a guard on both properties and let's not cock up again. This is personal so I won't be in a forgiving mood if we mess up. Now Juan Ramos is in charge and he'll brief you all."

George stormed out. He was angry, but not just with his men. He had promised Sam and Eddie he would look after them, he felt he had personally let them down. Juan followed him out. "Sir, they've found a stolen black Astra in Stanmore. Fits the description given by Eddie. Do you think there is a connection with Stanmore. That's where they're going."

"Look Juan. Maybe but it's a long shot. Perhaps he just chose Stanmore because he didn't want to use the A1 and he could get back into London. He knows the area; he had a house in Harrow. Maybe it's a coincidence; there'll be enough men. If I know Sam she won't go to a safe house or a hotel. Leave the plan as it is but tell the guys what you told me."

***

Juan Ramos walked around the Astra. It had been fingerprinted and checks were being made but he knew apart from the rental company and the couple from Iowa there were bound to be Bill's prints; he was certain. There was something about Bill's situation that meant he was on a crusade whatever the outcome, so he might have got careless. Juan was told the couple who had rented the car seemed to be enjoying the attention paid by the police. They'd not seen so much excitement for years.

"Sir." One of his men approached. "There is a TV crew here. I have no idea why, I think they were passing and saw all our cars. Will you have a word?"

Juan knew this was a bad idea but thought the speculation that might occur if he did not speak could be worse. "Okay but just for a couple of minutes."

A cameraman walked over with a reporter.

"We are in Stanmore where today a stolen car was left abandoned. Officer, can you tell us what has happened?"

"I'm afraid not. This car was reported stolen earlier today and we are checking to see whether it has been used in a crime. As of now we have no evidence to say that it was, so it might be just a routine car theft."

"It seems rather a large police presence for a simple car theft."

"That's as maybe but we have nothing further to add. If you will forgive me I have matters to attend to."

The reporter signed off his piece to camera stating the he had been talking to Sergeant Ramos of the Metropolitan Police.

Juan was relieved they had not been asked why it was not being dealt with by local police and rang Strachan to report.

***

Eddie and the family arrived at Sam's mum's house with unmarked police cars in front and behind and already parked across the road. He was driving the family car, the Porsche had already been impounded in the search for evidence. There must be a bullet lodged somewhere but Eddie could not see it. As they got out Violet came out with a worried expression. He assumed he was to blame for putting her daughter and grandchildren in danger. To his surprise she came over and clutched him to her and said, "Thank God you're okay. I don't know what I'd do if I lost another man in the family."

Eddie was shocked but delighted and a little emotional. He couldn't speak so he kissed Violet on the cheek and hugged her back. The kids were whisked inside and once the door was shut the cars that had travelled with them departed.

Sam asked Eddie into the garden for a quiet word. "Darling, I haven't said anything but if anything had happened to you today I don't know what I would have done. If harm comes to you or the kids I will personally kill Millichip."

Eddie looked at her. He believed her; after all, she was a competent and trained policewoman, although in her current condition he was not sure what she could do.

"Look, it was a narrow escape and it was partly my fault. Let's park it."

"I need to tell you something. I've kept this from you because… well, just because. When you were shot I ran and hid. One of his men came after me. He found me and we fought. He pinned me down and tried to rape me. Somehow I grabbed his gun and shot him."

"Jeez…. Why tell me now?"

"Two reasons. I want you to know I'll do anything to protect those I love and so you know I can."

"I sort of never doubted it but don't you think being a mother is enough. If something happened to me the kids need you alive not dead!"

"When you were shot at it brought it home to me. I'd sort of parked it."

"Would this explain the spent bullet casing in your drawer?"

"When did you find it?"

"When we moved to the new house."

"Why didn't you say anything?"

"I assumed you would tell me if you wanted me to know."

"Eddie you're the limit. Well you know now, is there anything else you want to know?'

"Absolutely nothing until Bill Millichip is caught and banged up."

Juan Ramos had no idea he was being followed. As he drove to Stanmore to brief Sam he did not see the Mini behind. It was the reporter and his cameraman. They knew there was more to this story and so had tracked him since they had filed their report.

Juan arrived and Eddie answered the door. He ushered him in and was greeted as always like one of the family. The cameraman had a clear shot of Eddie and panned back to show the house and the neighbouring properties. It was within a stone's throw of the Leefe Robinson Beefeater Inn. They decided to move away to download their piece to the newsroom. They had no idea what would be done with their work.

Later that evening, Bill was sitting in an Internet café searching the web for some information on cancers. He really had little idea what to look for as he had only felt generally unwell and weaker with occasional sickness. He switched over to live BBC London news feed and within a few moments a report came on about a stolen Astra found in Stanmore. He immediately recognised Ramos but couldn't understand why he was in England. It was not good news. It confirmed to him the case against him was fully open, but he expected nothing less. Then he thought he saw Eddie Jacobs standing at the front door of a house. Ramos had entered the house and the camera panned and he could see the Leefe Robinson Pub. He knew exactly where Eddie and his family had been moved.

Chapter 21

Jamie sat in his chair looking out at the street that for so long had been a dangerous place for him. So much had changed in his life. He thought about the night he had killed his father. He could not bring himself to remorse. His father had done nothing for him or his mother. How he missed her. All those years but still he felt pain; but life was different, better now. He had control of his life. He could go out, he had made contact with Ruth. It couldn't lead anywhere but it was cathartic. It put in place a part of his earlier life that for a fleeting moment had been good. Where would that meeting now lead?

He had not expected to meet Sam, how could he? It was chance in a million. He hadn't let on he'd a crush on her at school. Now would this be his first mistake? Could the chance meeting lead to a connection with his attack on their teacher. He needed to find out more about Sam Jacobs.

He sat at the computer and typed her name into Google and expected absolutely nothing. He was shocked at the number of references to her. She had been a policewoman and a famous name. He sat glued reading the press releases and background articles on her father and his tragic death. He spotted the name of George Strachan, the policeman he had tried to save before he was killed. Something registered in his mind but he could not think why. He read on and found that Sam had received a medal for the part she had played in a Peruvian drugs bust. It was fascinating but it worried Jamie.

From a meeting with Ruth which he knew could be risky as she was working with the police he had now become associated with another policewoman, who although no longer active could link him to his recent past activity. He sat back puzzling about what he had read and it struck him like thunderbolt. Strachan was the man in charge of his father's murder. A cold sweat came over him and he started to panic. He needed to get rid of any incriminating paperwork he had kept. This would include getting rid of his mum's photos and papers. He would not be able to part with the precious last letter his mum had written; he would have to find a safe place for that.

He would buy a good shredder and go through everything that might tie him into the killing.

***

"How did your meeting go with…?

"Jamie?" Ruth was caught off guard; she hadn't seen George standing by the coffee machine. "Fine. It was really eerie seeing your past again, bit creepy but fine. I'm glad I went and guess what?"

"I'm a copper but I need something more to go on."

"Sam knew Jamie."

"Knew him? How?"

"Went to school with him; at 15ish. Said he disappeared after his mother died. Didn't have a father. Thought he just left before his exams. He had been top of his class; expected to do well and just disappeared."

"Did he elaborate?"

"Only that he had been bullied and named a teacher. Can't remember the name but Sam does. Why the interest?

"I'm a policeman and anyone who contacts or knows Sam I want to know about. I'm her guardian angel, simple as that."

"Well, I'm sure she'd tell you more if you want to know."

"Anyway, you're ok about your meeting with Jamie. Will you meet again?"

"Yes, thanks, and no."

George wandered back to his office and jotted Jamie's name on his pad.

***

Bill sat drinking a pint in a grotty pub off the Edgware Road. He was assessing what his next move might be. He had enough cash to last him for a while provided he was careful. He had a gun; it weighed heavy in his jacket. It was hot outside, one of those airless humid days in London where it was better in than out. A fan was set up in the corner and every ten seconds he got the benefit of breeze. He was alone in the bar and the barmaid walked outside for a smoke. He would need another set of wheels if he was going to get Eddie or better still if he could get to Sam.

He walked down Edgware Road and turned into a side street. He could not believe his luck. A woman was delivering some dresses into an alterations shop and had left the engine running. It was a smart Audi and within seconds Bill was driving away with his new wheels. He smiled to himself as he drove to an area in Willesden where he knew a motor spares shop would give him a set of new plates without the necessary paperwork. An hour later he was driving around in a car that unless he was unlucky would escape detection for a few days.

He backtracked towards town and drove past Eddie's office. This was bad news, it was clear there were both marked and unmarked police cars staking the area. He then headed north towards Stanmore and as he headed west along Uxbridge Road he again spotted at least three cars in the vicinity of where Sam and Eddie were staying. This was going to very difficult. He drove to a hillside overlooking Harrow with a commanding view over London. He had often taken girlfriends there when he lived in the area. What an age ago that was. He sat thinking and lit a cigarette. He hadn't smoked for years. Something earlier in the day had prompted him to get cigarettes out of the machine in the pub and in his current predicament smoking was the least of his problems. He thought about the last few weeks and how this would all end. In all probability, it would not go well. Everything was stacked against him; no contacts, no access to more cash and an unknown diagnosis as to what might be wrong with him.

He had trusted his old doctor. He would not have sent him to Buenos Aries unless it was really important; but that decision to go had turned his world upside down. He could have spent his days at the estancia and the anger he felt toward Eddie Jacobs and Sam ought to have been bearable. "Too late now," he sighed looking at his face in the car mirror. God he looked awful. Either it was the mirror or he was definitely getting a grey pallor.

He took out his mobile. He wanted to say sorry to Elaine. She didn't deserve to be ripped off and he genuinely liked her. The phone kept ringing and he was about to end the call when she answered.

"Who is it?"

"Bill Millichip."

"You've got a bloody nerve...."

"Hold on Elaine, let me explain."

"What's to explain? You come asking for help; a couple of shags and you piss off with a grand of my money. Want to say sorry do you?"

This was not the same Elaine who he'd met the other week. She must be seriously pissed off. "Elaine, listen for a moment will you. I know it was shitty thing to do but I was desperate. I will find a way of getting the money back to you, I promise." He had no idea why he said that. He had no intention of doing so but if it made her feel better for the moment that was enough. He wanted to know if she had done anything about the missing money. "Did you report me?"

"Who to, the Cops? What do you think I am? Don't want them traipsing through my house thanks." There was a pause and Bill could sense there was something else coming. "I told Geoff."

"I bet he was thrilled."

"You may think it's funny but he's made some calls – so you'd better watch out. Now get lost."

The phone went dead. "That went well." He muttered but at least he found out what he wanted to know. He patted the gun in his jacket pocket.

***

"Gemma, get me Dick Williamson on the phone please."

"He's in the office."

George walked out and saw him by the window. "Dick, can you spare a minute?"

"What's up Guv?" this was Dick's standard response to being summoned.

"The Michael's murder, any developments?"

"Nothing Guv. Still no luck with an I/D from the cameras, nothing from the Sandwich shop, nor the footprint. Whilst we've no proof the murderer was known to Michaels ... he opened the door; it wasn't forced, so it's likely. Then there's the stabbings after the man had died, why do that? Rage? Let's assume the murderer actually knew his victim; but why kill him, was he out to get revenge? We know a person followed him home a number of times. I'm guessing the murderer was much younger than him; I know this is off the wall but what if he was a friend of the family?"

"What if he was family?"

"Michaels had no family."

George thought for a moment. "Come into the office."

"I know this sounds strange but what if Michaels had a son but didn't know."

"Excuse me Guv, but that's a bit off the wall isn't it?" He flinched inwardly at having said "'off the wall' again.

"I'm clutching at straws but suppose a son traced him and wanted to meet him; become acknowledged?"

"What you mean the old man rejected him and the son kills him?"

"The reason I'm floating this is that I heard something about a young lad who Sam Jacobs knew at school, who had no father and when his mum died he went to pieces. There is absolutely no obvious connection but I want you to find out anything on a Jamie Smith, mid to late 30's, and I think Ruth says he said he lived south of the river."

"What's Ruth got to do with this?"

"Long story and don't go asking her about him please, not for the present."

Dick left the office and went to his desk. He sat thinking this was the most tenuous connection on which to base his investigation. 'Hey ho,' he mused, the boss has been great at breaking cases and what did he have, nothing.'

***

Jamie sat at the shredder and filled three bin liners with photos and correspondence from his mother's papers. He only kept photos of her and his aunt but any with his father would have to go. He went to his computer and trashed everything that had related to his searches to his father and Jacobson. He guessed experts would be able to recreate incriminating items but he wasn't about to dump his prized laptop. He was uncertain how to dispose of the bin liners. He had no idea whether shredded documents could be recreated but to burn them was not an option in his flat. He decided to take one at a time and to take them to different bins at the back of shops in the main High Street. That for now was all he could do. He was worried whether he was over reacting to the meeting with Ruth and Sam. Strangely it was Sam he was more concerned about; the link to Jacobson worried him.

George rang Sam. "How's my favourite lady?"

"Fat."

"When are you due?"

"Two weeks and if I'm not done they'll induce me."

"You feeling okay?"

"Bit worried, the shooting. He's getting close."

"He won't get any closer. I promise. Sam about that meeting with Ruth and Jamie."

"What about it?"

"What do you know about him?'

"Has Ruth said anything?"

"Only that you knew him from school, he was bullied and he mentioned a teacher."

"Jacobson. No idea what became of him? Nobody liked him. Austere, old-fashioned teacher, keen on punishment. Why."

"Nothing except where you are concerned I want to know everything and his sudden leaving is odd. You said he had no father."

"Yes. Kids can be cruel. He was a strange looking boy and people picked on him. Felt sorry in a way. A friend said he fancied me."

"But nothing happened?"

"Good lord, no."

"What school was it?"

"George, don't you think you are being a bit over zealous."

"I'll be the judge of that."

Sam had no idea what was in his mind but she told him and the conversation sort of petered out. After a pause he said goodbye and wished her and the baby well.

Sam thought that was the weirdest conversation she had ever had with him; she hoped he was not losing the plot.

***

George had told Williamson to include a search on Jacobson in his latest searches on Jamie. He wondered why the guv'nor thought there might be any link. Nothing had come up on Jamie at all. Never been in trouble to get himself on the radar. Jacobson however was different. Reports of violence and a call for him to be retired early or face dismissal. The files were incomplete but a quick search of records had shown him retired and living in Hatfield.

He approached Strachan's office and was surprised to see Sam and Eddie sitting opposite his boss. Everyone knew how crucial it was to keep these two safe. He had never actually spoken to Sam. She had been long retired before his transfer but he thought this new information might be pertinent as she was here.

He knocked and was motioned inside.

"This is Dick Williamson. Recently transferred from Tooting and dealing with the Michaels murder. What's up?"

"Well Sir. You asked me to find out about the teacher Jacobson and as Sam was here do you want me to brief you now?"

George was irritated. He didn't want to bother Sam but he knew he would have no choice. "Let's have it."

"Retired early after complaints from parents that he was overzealous in handing out punishments. Where is he now?"

"Hatfield."

"Dick, I want someone to go there and interview him. Come up with some story that we need his help, about an old student."

"We could say it was about me," Sam chipped in. I have no idea what Jamie has to do with anything but I had no issue with him and he may be more cooperative."

"Okay, on balance, Dick, go yourself, but liaise with Hatfield, don't want to offend anyone and they may have some useful information on him."

***

The next day Williamson arrived at Hertfordshire County HQ at Welwyn Garden City. The call to Hatfield local had been passed up to them. He teamed up with bright young police constable in uniform

"Hi. I'm Dick Williamson and you're Angie, is that right?"

"Yes Angie Holmes. What's this all about," she asked, flattered to be working with someone from New Scotland Yard, we know of nothing we should be concerned about. He's not on the paedophile register."

They drove to the address they were given.

"This goes back to when he was a teacher and was asked to retire after allegations of 'overzealous' use of the cane."

"What's that got to do with now?"

"Good question, to which I don't have a good answer. Just be supportive if he looks like he's scared. We only want to talk to see what he knows about a lad called Jamie Smith who he used to teach. Initially he's been told it is about a girl, Sam, at the same school and time. She's a police heroin and so we just want to ask what he knows about her and see where it leads."

They arrived at the bungalow and he was looking out the window. He opened the door as they walked down the path and they stepped inside. It was obvious he had lived alone for a long time. The place had the smell of an old man, stale, musty and totally devoid of warmth.

"I'm Detective Dick Williamson and this is my colleague Angie Holmes. It's very good of you to see us at short notice. There's absolutely no problem. Just want to see if you give us some background on one of your students. A girl, Sam Jones was her name and all this was 20 years ago. I know you must have taught thousands of kids but when we rang you said you remembered her."

"Clear as a bell. Bright as a button she was. Really popular and I always thought she should do well. I know her father was policeman and I also read he was shot and she followed him into the police. I saw she was awarded a medal not long ago."

"You are well-informed."

"Take pride in seeing kids do well. Get hurt also when bright kids fail."

"Expect there were a few of those."

"Not as many as you would expect. I had one kid who could have got a scholarship to Oxford. His mum died and he went to pieces. No father either."

"Do you remember his name?"

"I didn't but it came back to me some weeks ago. I was walking through the woods at the back and I thought I was being followed. I might look old but I'm not afraid. I hid and then crept back to where I last heard the noise and blow me one of my old students was standing there. He shouted at me then I panicked and tried to hit him with my stick. We scuffled and he ran off."

Dick wanted to let him continue but Angie asked "Do you know who it was?"

"A lad called Jamie. Smith I think, yes Jamie Smith."

"Did you report this?"

"Hell no. Don't wish to be rude but I'm not a great fan of you lot. You must have checked that I was retired early. 'Overzealous use of the cane' I was told. Jamie said I'd ruined his life but the way he scarpered I knew I wouldn't see him again and frankly I'm too old to be explaining my actions of 20 years ago. I was a good teacher."

"You don't know whether he lives locally?

"Sorry."

"How did he find you?"

"Well, that's odd because a few weeks before I had one of those calls out of the blue – said it was some marketing company, asked if I was Mr Jacobson, I said yes and I told them to get lost and they put the phone down. Maybe he'd tracked down Jacobson's in the phone book until he was sure I was the right one. How he came to look in Hatfield I've no idea."

Williamson knew all he needed to know. As a policeman there were lots of other questions he could ask but he could do that later if needed. He wanted to get back.

"I'm going to give you a card and if you think of anything that might be helpful give us a ring."

They shook hands with the old man. He had been alive during the interview as though he was looking forward to it and now it was over he was a nobody again.

"Well, that led directly to where you wanted but how does it help?"

"Angie, it tells us here is Jamie who was interested in finding some person who had bullied him. It looks likely he was after revenge; he might have attacked Jacobson had he not surprised him. Maybe he did that to someone else and that's what we, sorry I have to piece together. Thanks for your help – do you want to go back to the office?"

"No. I have some business here in Hatfield and I'll cadge a lift back later. Just down here will do."

He watched as Angie walked into a small parade of shops. He rang Strachan to debrief him.

"Well done Dick. We'll have to ratchet up this lead on Jamie. By the way ring HQ and thank the DS for his help."

"Already done so. See you later, what's next?"

"Debrief at 9 tomorrow."

Dick liked being part of Strachan's team, infinitely better than Tooting.

***

He arrived early at the briefing room to prepare. The squad appeared just before nine and Strachan strode into the room.

"OK. The Michaels murder. It's a long shot but we may have a new lead. A chance meeting between Sam Jacobs and a young man called Jamie Smith has opened up a line of enquiry that is definitely worth pursuing. Dick feels that Michaels' murderer knew him even if Michaels did not know his murderer. That could be because something had happened in the past and he might have tracked Michaels down to get some revenge or whatever.

We know that the sandwich bar assistant spotted this man and we know he was caught on CCTV; in all probability he was being stalked. This man could be Jamie Smith but it is a long shot. Sam Jacobs told us Jamie had no known father and when his mother died he ducked out of school. He was top of his class and bright but was bullied, not least by his teacher. The coincidence is that Sam went to school with this lad and knew of the teacher concerned. His name is Jacobson who was retired early for excessive use of the cane. Dick traced him to Hatfield and interviewed him yesterday. Dick you take it on."

"I saw him and he told me of a chance encounter he had with Jamie who had tracked him to Hatfield and was following him through a wood. The old man, feisty guy for his age, realised someone was there and surprised this Jamie. There was a scuffle and Jamie ran off and the old man never bothered to report the incident. What the Guv'nor thinks is if he has done this once perhaps Jamie had done it before. The theory is…" Dick looked for a nod to proceed, "We think Michaels could have been Jamie's father."

The tension in the room had grown. "It's tenuous," Strachan picked up the thread, "but if in his mother's papers he had been able to identify Frank Michaels as a possible father he might have tracked him by some process and confronted him. God knows why he then went on to attack the man. Presumably Michaels wanted nothing to do with him and the reason he stabbed him repeatedly after the man had died could have been rage, frustration, whatever. What we now have is a lead to follow. Dick has provided some notes and a description of Jamie, he's not on file but we want to talk to him. Any questions?"

Murmurs but no questions. "Dick you run this search for Jamie. Priority, guys, might be a long shot but what else do we have."

Chapter 22

Jamie had been thinking his mad decision to meet with Ruth was a disaster. The chance meeting with Sam, a former policewoman and a former classmate was one thing but to get onto the topic of Jacobson could have serious consequences. He had now removed all evidence from his flat but instincts told him he might have to move on. He would leave for now and if nothing happened in the next few weeks he would return. He packed a small rucksack and with his laptop he left. He had no idea where he was going but he stopped at a cash machine and drew out £250. He could go and stay in a small hotel somewhere or maybe he should get far away from London. Abroad was not an option; he had never bothered to get a passport. He didn't even have a full driving licence; he'd only ever qualified for a motorbike. He might buy a small second hand motorbike or even a moped just to keep mobile.

That evening he emerged from a bike shop in Balham with a 125cc Honda and a crash hat, which was all he needed. He wobbled at first but was soon riding fairly confidently. The summer was proving hot and stifling in London and out of town was much more comfortable. He nearly stopped at a small hotel but it was such a warm evening he parked in a field and decided to spend the night 'al fresco'. He had no real idea where he was. His only journeys had been by public transport; this was a whole new experience. He felt exhilarated and not at all scared; but sleep eluded him. His mind was active. Above all was the desire not to be caught but also he was starting to feel remorse for his actions.

That morning he started off and the first signs he saw were A1 North, Hatfield. This was not a good idea so he turned off west towards Elstree and Stanmore.

***

Bill Millichip had decided what to do next. He was being hunted by the police and had no idea how much time he had left to get his revenge. He started the Audi. His back ached from sleeping in the car. He backed out of the car park on onto Old Redding Lane and towards Stanmore. He was going to make something happen today.

***

Strachan and Williamson arrived outside Jamie's flat in an unmarked car. Two other cars were parked close by. An Armed Detective accompanied them and they rang the tradesmen's buzzer and the entrance door clicked open. Williamson had done a great job in tracing Jamie's flat. With all his local knowledge and contacts it had taken only a couple of hours.

They walked cautiously up the stairs. They were almost certain Jamie was not armed but caution kept you alive.

They knocked on the door but there was no answer. A man poked his head out of a door, which looked like a cupboard.

"You looking for Jamie?"

"Do you know where he is?"

"He went out with a bag yesterday afternoon. Never goes anywhere. Thought it a bit odd. Who are you?"

"Police. Do you know anyone who can let us in?"

"I'm the janitor, I could but you got a warrant?"

"We can get one but just open up, we want a look inside."

The janitor came and with a bunch of keys opened the door. "Hope this doesn't get me in trouble?"

"Not from us it won't."

They walked in leaving the janitor in the corridor. It was a tastefully furnished flat with a bedroom, lounge kitchen and modern bathroom and spotlessly clean. An extensive search revealed nothing.

Strachan went outside and the janitor was waiting. "Thanks for being so helpful. Here's a number to ring if Jamie comes back but I don't want you telling him we've been here, understood."

"What's he done?"

"Nothing, we just want to talk to him."

They went outside none the wiser as to whether Jamie was really a suspect in the Michaels case. Williamson was convinced and Strachan was increasingly of that opinion.

***

Bill drove past the house where Sam was staying with her mother. There was no car outside in the drive, nor from what he could see was there any police presence. This might present him with an opportunity. He parked about half a mile away and walked to the house.

Was this a good idea? Probably not, but he had to force the pace whatever the outcome. He walked up to the front door and rung the bell, his hand on the gun in his pocket. Nobody answered. He stood there for a full two minutes more to find out if there was any police presence. He walked to the side gate; there was no lock so he went to the back door. It was locked. Even for him he was tense. He picked up a large pebble surrounding a flowerbed and smashed the glass. The window fell in and on to carpet so there was no great noise.

He waited for a minute before he put his hand through and found the key was in the door. He went inside and found himself in a utility room. No alarm had sounded but he was uncertain what might happen when he opened the door to what turned out to be the kitchen. Silence. His heart rate slowed and he was figuring out what he would do if the family returned. There was the mother and kids as well as Sam and the police would be outside, worse still they might come in the house with them. Then he would have one option, shoot Sam and see if he could shoot his way out past the police almost certainly armed after his attempt on Eddie.

"Armed Police." Bill froze; now he would have to take his chances. He had no idea if there was one or a hundred.

"Come out with your hands on your head."

Bill moved through to the dining room facing the street and could only see one car and nobody around. Perhaps it was just one policeman. He decided to go out of the front door. Maybe they were at the side gate. He opened the door and there was a policeman running around from the gate. Bill instinctively fired and the man fell clutching his side. He raced across the street towards his car. Nobody followed. He got back to his car and was convulsed in coughing. He was bringing up phlegm but when he looked there was blood on his handkerchief.

Chapter 23

Jamie was now depressed. He did not realise how safe he had felt in his flat. He was on the run, but actually had no idea whether anyone was chasing him! He had this gnawing at his insides. He was no natural killer. He had planned revenge but not cold blooded murder; but then his father was dying of a heart attack when he had lost control and started stabbing him. So what to do now?

He needed to explain for the sake of his own conscience. He knew he would not survive in prison so the only alternatives were to keep running but how long would he last. It was midsummer and he had only spent one sleepless night sleeping rough.

He could commit suicide as an alternative to being caught but did he have the courage? More than anything he wanted to get it off his chest. He knew only two people, Sam, not a good choice and Ruth. Ruth might understand and sympathise, she might have suggestions as to what to do.

He would try and locate her through her website.

He logged on that evening from an Internet café. There was a contact e-mail site. He sent her a message saying he had to speak to her once more before he went away. To his surprise he got an out of office e-mail with a contact mobile phone number. He dialled the number and got a message service. He left no message. He wanted only to speak to decide what to do next. At about 8 o'clock that evening he rang and she answered.

"Hi Ruth. This is Jamie. I hope you don't mind but I found your number on your website."

A cautious Ruth said, "What do you want Jamie?"

"I'm in trouble and I want your advice."

Bill drove past the house. It was a crazy risk but he wanted to see the outcome. As yet there was no ambulance or other police cars but a passer-by was trying to help the injured policeman.

He drove further towards Stanmore and then he spotted Sam's BMW X5, she was coming out of a shop with bags to put in the car. The tailgate was up and nobody else was in the car. He jammed on his brakes and slid the car behind her. She was startled and then the recognition; a look of terror spread across her face. He was out of his Audi and bundled her into the back of the car. She was about to scream but he hit her hard and no sound came out of her mouth. She was limp in his arms and he shoved her in and slammed the tailgate and got in the driver's seat. The keys were in the ignition. He started and pulled out knocking over a cyclist and pulled across the traffic and sideswiped a woman in a Mini pulling out from the other side of the road.

He could see the carnage in his mirror as he accelerated away. He knew he would have to act fast. Maybe her protection detail had been called to the house or maybe they would be in pursuit. He drove for a mile and turned up a country lane and soon saw a barn. It was disused with no doors and half the roof missing but ideal for his purpose. He killed the engine and pulled Sam out of the back. He dragged her roughly across the dirt floor before propping her up against a large post. She was coming around and he stood facing her.

"You are going to die. You have caused me too much trouble and now I have nothing to live for. I've lost everything and now I'm dying. But you first."

Sam was powerless to do anything. In her state she could not move quickly to stop him or even get out of the way. She thought of Eddie and her darling children.

Then he raised the gun and the shot reverberated around the barn. Sam lay there thinking why doesn't this hurt? Then Bill toppled forward clutching his leg. Two men appeared at the door.

Thank God, thought Sam the police, but she could see the two men were not policemen. One kicked Bill's gun away and rolled him over on his back. They stared down at him.

"That was for Geoff and the next one is for Elaine. He knelt down and rifled Bill's pockets. They were empty.

"Elaine's money is in an Audi I left when I snatched her. So it's gone."

With that he put his gun in Bill's mouth and blew his brains out. She had seen a number of people being shot, but never at such close range. The blood was horrendous but it was so final. No writhing in pain. One second Millichip was about to kill her and the next second he was dead.

"Lady we know what you did to Bill but that's none of our business. This is a private score. Get in your car and go."

She tried to scramble to her feet but could not get up. Oddly, she thought to herself, one of the men helped her up gently and guided her to the car. She eased into the driver's seat and locked the doors and started the engine. She was terrified rather than elated at seeing the man she feared most being shot. She had spent all this time dreading him coming after them and now she could not convince herself it was possibly all over. There had to be something more.

She backed out and before she reached the main road she punched in Strachan's number on the phone. Her hands were now trembling and she felt faint. "God, I hope this doesn't bring the baby on." She finally rang Strachan. She knew he would be able to trace the call.

Strachan answered immediately.

"George, I got snatched by Bill at the shops."

"Yes, I know. We have your location and a team will be there in five minutes. Are you safe, are you hurt?"

"I'm fine but I need to leave. Two men came and shot Bill just before he was about to shoot me."

She looked in the mirror as she got to the gate and the two men were dousing the barn in petrol. This brought her to her senses. Within a minute it would be ablaze. How ironic she thought; Bill had tried to kill her and Eddie by setting a barn on fire.

"They're torching the barn, so I need to be out of here before they leave and have second thoughts about letting me go. I'm going to Mum's."

"Bit hectic there with an officer shot but okay, I'll tell them you're coming back. Eddie will be on his way, I told him about the break-in at your Mum's but he obviously is unaware Bill snatched you. I need to kill this call; I'll be down to see you within the hour. Bye. It's over now. Bill can't hurt you now."

The phone went dead but all Sam wanted was a friendly, reassuring voice to talk to.

As she arrived at her mother's house there were so many cars she could not park. She left it in the road and there were the kids with her mother hopefully oblivious to what she had just endured. Strachan and Eddie were on the way but Sam's first act after cuddling the kids was to put the kettle on.

The realisation now set in. Five years of worry, five years of looking over her shoulder were now finished. Bill was dead. He could no longer hurt her, Eddie or the kids. She broke down in tears and her Mum comforted her without asking for an explanation.

Within ten minutes, Eddie and Strachan arrived. Eddie held Sam in his arms and looked at the bruise that was forming on her face. George was impatient to hear what had happened. She explained it patiently.

"Who were these two?"

"Obviously friends of someone in Bill's outfit but clearly with a grudge."

"Geoff and Elaine? Is that who they said?"

"Yes."

"Geoff's doing time for armed robbery and was an acquaintance of Bill's and Elaine is his wife. No names of the other two?"

"No. They didn't introduce themselves and Bill had no time to indicate whether he knew them or not."

"OK, I've asked the paramedic who first got here to just check you over. That bruise on your face will need some attention."

"I'm OK."

"You'll do as you're told." Eddie said allowing for no argument.

Sam was in no mood for argument. She felt faint and collapsed in Eddie's arms.

***

Eddie sat down with Sam's mum once the kids were asleep.

"How much did Sam tell you about what happened in Peru?"

"Who knows with Sam, but most I guess, why?"

"It's just you seem to take all this in your stride."

"I stopped worrying about things I could do nothing about once Sam's father was killed. Then when she gave up nursing to join the force I thought it would put me in an early grave so George Strachan said he would look out for us both and I was not to worry so I didn't. George has been wonderful. He's full of guilt that he survived and... well you know."

"You certainly brought up one resourceful daughter. It clearly can't have been her fate to die today. Part of me hopes the two who shot Millichip get away with it, but Sam would disagree."

"She sure would. If they did it once they might do it again. And based on how they did it I suspect it's not the first time."

"Violet, will you come home with us and stay until the baby comes?"

"On one condition."

"What's that?"

"I'm mum, not Violet."

"Fair enough."

Chapter 24

Ruth was in awe of the telephone call she was having with Sam.

"When I was bundled into the car at first I had no idea it was Bill Millichip. He caught me from behind and as I turned round he hit me. I went out like a light. The next thing I remember is leaning against a post in a barn. I thought oh' no not a barn again. That will make three where I've been in threat of being killed. Nobody would help this time? Imagine two white knights, I don't care if they were villains, just appeared. I was looking into the light through the door so I couldn't see them clearly.

Then the shot. I really thought it was Bill and I could not understand why I felt nothing. In that instant I had a flash of Eddie and the kids, strangely I had no thought of the baby. Then he fell groaning. They could have killed him but they wanted him to know why they were there."

"Did they say anything?"

"Only one said anything. This is for Geoff and Elaine. That's all he said. Then he walked up, he had his back to me. He put the gun in Bill's mouth and shot him. The rest as they say is history. They told me to go, but I couldn't get up and one of them helped up and to the car and I didn't look back. I saw them setting light to the barn. I've no idea why but it might just be because he set fire to a barn when he held Eddie and me. Poetic justice maybe?"

"How are you feeling now?"

"Very relieved and the Doc says I'm fine. They are going to induce me next week."

"Nightmare over. What about writing a book about your experience. I'll help."

"Thanks but no thanks. I've a lovely life at home and thankful to be left alone. We're going to tour France next year, extended holiday. Vince told Eddie he needs a long break and he'll come back and run things. Enough about me how's you?"

"I had a call from Jamie."

"What did he want?"

"Say's he's in some form of bother and needs my advice."

"You're not going to see him are you? George believes he could be involved in some way in the Michaels' murder. Have you told George?"

"No and for the moment promise me Sam you won't either. Not until I find out what he wants to say."

"I can't Ruth. George is like a father to me. It would be a betrayal of all the trust we have in each other. I have to tell him."

"Then I won't see Jamie. I know it sounds strange but he saved my life. Nothing heroic but his kindness gave me a life, success – I couldn't do that to him."

"Promise me you won't meet him without having told George."

Promise me you won't tell George until I've rung Jamie and I won't meet him. I'll ring Jamie tonight and talk to him."

"If that's the best I can get, OK."

"I've got to go, there's a briefing. Keep me posted on the baby. Love to Eddie, bye."

Ruth wished she hadn't said anything. Now she would have to break a promise to Sam. She intended to meet Jamie. If she could help him it would repay a big debt in her mind. She doubted Sam could keep her part of the bargain either, her loyalty to the force and to George would scupper that, so she would contact Jamie that evening.

Ruth decided not to use her mobile and went to a pay phone in the Broadway Underground station. She rang the number he had given her and he answered immediately.

"Hi Jamie, it's Ruth. What is so important that you need to speak with me? Can't we do it over the phone I'm really busy," she lied.

"Can we meet? I need to chat and I promise it will be just this once. You said that I helped you once. Now I need your help."

"Are you in trouble with the police?"

"No," he lied.

"OK it's lovely evening. Let's meet on the Embankment, by Cleopatra's Needle at half past seven."

Jamie thought he could make that in time. He'd go on the bike. "OK I'll be there. I'm coming on my new motorbike. See you then."

Ruth had two hours to kill so she went home and showered. It had been a hot day and she was over dressed. She would put on a pair of cut-off jeans.

***

She arrived early at the spot and sat on a bench overlooking the Thames. The rush hour was slowing down and there were fewer people walking about, tourists mainly. She felt guilty at having lied to Sam and being disloyal to George. She was tempted to ring him but she owed Jamie one last meeting. He had sounded almost pathetic imploring her but she knew how this must have felt to him.

She was daydreaming and then suddenly there he was. He had sat down beside her. She had expected to hear a motorbike stop but had heard nothing.

"Thanks Ruth. I really need to talk."

"Sounds dramatic, Jamie."

"It is. You said that you reached the depths of despair once. Well it's not like that for me. I have done something which I now regret but can't face the consequences."

"You'd better spell it out. Let's see what you might need to do about it."

"I killed Frank Michaels."

Ruth thought she must have misheard him. "Come again – you did what?"

"I found out he was almost certainly my father. I tracked him down from papers my mother left when she died. I was going through a terrible time. I had been badly beaten up near my home and I decided I needed to get revenge somehow. I followed him home a few times then one night I knocked on his door and barged in to confront him. I only had a heavy torch with me, no other weapon but the worst bit, I can't really come to terms with is I really think I went there with the intention of killing him."

Ruth wanted to ask questions but decided to let it all pour out.

"He fought me and I hit him with the torch and he started to collapse with a heart attack. He died on the floor right there without me finding out definitely he was my father. He hadn't denied knowing mum and the dates of their friendship were right so I was pretty sure but seeing him dead I lost it. Denied seeing him suffer for all the hurt he caused mum and me I picked up some big heavy scissors and stabbed him over and over again. When I realised what I had done I cleaned up and got out of there and destroyed clothing, shoes, anything that could tie me in and went home. For a while I was shocked but quite proud of regaining control of my life."

"Jamie I don't know what to say."

"I can't own up and go to prison, it would kill me being locked up."

All of a sudden out of the corner of her eye Ruth saw movement.

"Police. We are armed. Stay where you are and raise your hands. Miss move away slowly."

Ruth stood and moved cautiously away from the bench. Jamie stood with his hands in the air and turned to face the policemen. Then he deliberately reached down to his jacket. Two consecutive shots rang out and he fell to the floor beside Ruth.

Ruth screamed. "Jamie, why?"

She knelt down and cradled his head in her lap. Blood was flowing from chest wounds. "Call an ambulance," she shrieked.

She looked down at his face. He knew this was the end and he looked happy his ordeal was over. All he said was "Thank you Ruth," and he died in her arms.

Epilogue

Sam lay contented, cradling baby George in her arms. Eddie sat by the bedside with Violet who was keeping the kids as quiet as it was possible to do.

"All's well that ends well," Sam muttered to herself.

"What?"

"Nothing. I was just thinking how tame and quiet, almost orderly our life will be without Bill Millichip. We'll have to find some other excitement."

Violet rolled her eyes and Eddie just smiled. "For now let's just be thankful you and George are both OK."

"George rang to wish you well," Violet chipped in, "he's tickled pink that you named him George. He was really emotional. Your friend Ruth rang and said if she can she'd like to come over and see you."

"Oh yes, tell her to come this afternoon, or anytime but make it before we get discharged. I'm dying to know how her phone call with Jamie went."

"Sam," Eddie interrupted, "Jamie is dead. Ruth actually met him and George had been suspicious and had Ruth watched. An armed response team shot him when they think he went for a gun in his jacket. There was no gun so it looks as though Jamie forced them to kill him. He had told Ruth that he killed Frank Michaels."

Eddie briefly told her the story. Sam was saddened. "Poor Ruth. Finding Jamie had meant so much too her. I must talk to her. I hope she didn't think that I broke my promise."

"And two more pieces of news. George has been promoted to Superintendent and Juan has been asked to return to Peru to stand as a member of their Congress. He will be leaving in two weeks so you'll have a chance to meet with him. There will be a big celebration at George's later next week."

Sam choked back a tear. "I shall be so sorry to not have Juan around but he is needed back home. Eddie we can go to see him there..."

Made in the USA
Charleston, SC
04 January 2016